Christmas in Manhattan

All the drama of the ER, all the magic of Christmas!

A festive welcome to Manhattan Mercy ER, a stone's throw from Central Park in the heart of New York City. Its reputation for top-notch health care is eclipsed only by the reputation of the illustrious, wealthy Davenport family and the other dedicated staff who work there!

With snow about to blanket New York over Christmas, ER chief Charles Davenport makes sure his team is ready for the drama and the challenge...but when it comes to love, a storm is coming as they've never seen before!

Available now:

Sleigh Ride with the Single Dad by Alison Roberts

Dr. Grace Forbes is reunited with old flame Charles Davenport—but will the brooding father and his adorable twins make her Christmas dreams come true?

A Firefighter in Her Stocking by Janice Lynn

Dr. Sarah Grayson can't resist a festive fling with her playboy neighbor, hunky firefighter Jude Davenport, even if she knows she's playing with fire...

And coming soon:

The Spanish Duke's Holiday Proposal by Robin Gianna
The Rescue Doc's Christmas Miracle by Amalie Berlin
Christmas with the Best Man by Susan Carlisle
Navy Doc on Her Christmas List by Amy Ruttan

SLEIGH RIDE WITH THE SINGLE DAD

ALISON ROBERTS

HARLEQUIN MEDICAL ROMANCE™

Recycling programs
for this product may
not exist in your area.

Special thanks and acknowledgment are given
to Alison Roberts for her contribution to the
Christmas in Manhattan series.

ISBN-13: 978-0-373-21556-0

Sleigh Ride with the Single Dad

First North American Publication 2017

Copyright © 2017 by Harlequin Books S.A.

HARLEQUIN®
www.Harlequin.com

Printed in U.S.A.

CHAPTER ONE

As an omen, this wasn't good.

It could have been the opening scene to a horror movie, in fact.

Grace Forbes, in her crisp, clean set of scrubs—her stethoscope slung around her neck along with the lanyard holding her new Manhattan Mercy ID card—walking towards Charles Davenport who, as chief of Emergency Services, was about to give her an official welcome to her new job.

An enormous clap of thunder rolled overhead from a storm that had to be directly on top of central New York and big enough for the sound to carry into every corner of this huge building.

And then the lights went out.

Unexpectedly, the moment Grace had been bracing herself for became an anti-climax. It was no longer important that this was the first time in more than a decade that her path was about to cross with that of the man who'd rocked her world back in the days of Harvard Medical School. Taking control of a potential crisis in a crowded emergency room was the only thing that mattered.

In the brief, shocked silence that followed both the clap of thunder, a terrified scream from a child and the startling contrast of a virtually windowless area bathed in bright, neon lighting being transformed instantly into the shadowed gloom of a deep cave, Charles Davenport did exactly that.

'It's just a power outage, folks.' He raised his voice but still sounded calm. 'Stay where you are. The emergency generators will kick in any minute.'

Torch apps on mobile phones flickered on like stars appearing in a night sky and beams of light began to sweep the area as people tried to see what was going on. The noise level rose and rapidly got louder and louder. Telephones were ringing against the backdrop of the buzz of agitated conversations. Alarms sounded to warn of the power disruption to medical equipment. Staff, including the administrative clerks from the waiting area, triage nurses and technicians were moving towards the central desk to await instructions and their movements triggered shouts from people desperate for attention.

'Hey, come back…where are you going?'

'Help…I need *help*.'

'Nurse…over *here*…please?'

'I'm scared, Mommy…I want to go *home*…'

Grace stayed where she was, her gaze fixed on Charles. The dramatic change in the lighting had softened the differences that time had inevitably produced and, for a heartbeat, he looked exactly as he had that night. Exactly like the haunting figure that had walked through her mind and her heart so often when sleep had opened portals to another time.

Tall and commanding. Caring enough to come after her and find out what was wrong so he could do something about making it better…

Which was pretty much what he was doing right now. She could see him assessing the situation and dealing with the most urgent priorities, even as he took in information that was coming at him from numerous directions.

'Miranda—check any alarms coming from cardiac monitors.'

'Get ready to put us on bypass for incoming patients. If we don't get power back on fast, we'll have a problem.'

'Put the trauma team on standby. If this outage is widespread, we could be in for a spate of accidents.'

Sure enough, people manning the telephones and radio links with the ambulance service were already taking calls.

'Traffic lights out at an intersection on Riverside Drive. Multi-vehicle pile-up. Fire service called for trapped patients. Cyclist versus truck incoming, stat.'

'Fall down stairs only two blocks away. Possible spinal injury. ETA two minutes.'

'Estates need to talk to you, Dr Davenport. Apparently there's some issue with the generators and they're prioritising Theatres and ICU…'

Charles nodded tersely and began issuing orders rapidly. Staff dispersed swiftly to cover designated areas and calm patients. A technician was dispatched to find extra batteries that might be needed for backup for equipment like portable ultrasound and X-ray machines. Flashlights were found and given to orderlies, security personnel and even patients' relatives to hold. Finally, Charles had an instruction specifically directed to Grace.

'Come with me,' he said. 'I need someone to head the trauma team if I have to troubleshoot other stuff.' He noticed heads turning in his direction. 'This is Dr Grace Forbes,' he announced briskly. 'Old colleague of mine who's come from running her own emergency department in outback Australia. She probably feels right at home in primitive conditions like this.'

A smile or two flashed in Grace's direction as her new workmates rushed past to follow their own orders. The smile Charles gave her was distinctly wry. Because of the unusual situation she was being thrown into? Or was it because he knew that describing her as an old colleague was stretching the truth more than a little? It was true that she and Charles had worked in the same hospital more than once in that final year of medical school but their real relationship had been that of fierce but amicable rivals for the position of being the top student of their year. The fact that Charles knew where she'd been recently, when he hadn't been present for the interview she'd had for this job, was another indication that he was on top of his position of being head of this department.

No wonder he'd won that final battle of the marks, even though it had only been by a small margin.

'Welcome to Manhattan Mercy, Grace… Trauma One is this way…'

It was hardly the best way to welcome a new member of staff but maybe it was better this way, with so many things to think about that Charles couldn't allow any flashes of memory to do more than float past the edges of his conscious mind.

He hadn't seen Grace since he'd noticed her in the audience when he'd walked onto the stage to accept the trophy for being the top student of their graduation party from medical school.

He hadn't spoken to her since…since *that* night…

'Warn people that waiting times are going to go through the roof for anything non-urgent,' he told the senior member of the administrative team as he passed her. 'But don't push them out the door. By the sound of this storm, it's not safe out there.'

A flicker in the ambient light filtering into the department suggested a flash of lightning outside and another roll of thunder could be heard only a second later so they were still right underneath it. Fingers crossed that the worst of the storm would cross the central city quickly but how long would it be before the power disruption was sorted? And how many problems would it cause?

The weather alone would give them a huge spike in traffic accidents. A sudden plunge into darkness could cause all sorts of trauma like that fall down stairs already on its way. And what about the people on home oxygen who could find themselves in severe respiratory distress with the power outage cutting off their support? They needed to be ready for anything in the ER and he needed to clear space for the potential battleground of dodging unexpected missiles of incoming cases and whatever ambush could be in store with equipment that might not be functioning until power came back on.

He hadn't faced a challenge like this for a long time but he had learned way back how to multi-task when the proverbial was hitting the fan and Charles knew he could function effectively on different levels at the same time.

Like knowing which patients could be sidelined for observation well away from centrestage and directing staff members to transfer them as he passed their ed cubicles at the same time as fending off a request from a television crew who happened to be in the area and wanted to cover the fallout from what was apparently a record-breaking storm.

'Keep them out of here,' he growled. 'We're going to have more than enough to deal with.'

It never took long for the media to get their teeth into something, did it? Memories of how much damage had been done to his own family all those years ago had left Charles with a mistrust bordering on paranoia. It was a time of his life he had no desire to revisit so it was perhaps unfortunate that the arrival of Grace Forbes in his department had the ability to stir those memories.

And others...

A glance over his shoulder showed him that Grace was following his slightly circuitous route to Trauma One as he made sure he knew what was happening everywhere at the moment. The expression on her face was serious and the focus in those dark grey eyes reminded him of how capable he knew she was. And how intelligent. He'd had to fight hard back at medical school to keep his marks on the same level as Grace and, while they'd never moved in the same social circles, he'd had enormous respect for her. A respect that had tipped into something very different when he'd discovered that she had a vulnerable side, mind you, but he wasn't going to allow the memory of that night to surface.

No way. Even if this situation wasn't making it completely unacceptable to allow such a personal distraction, he wouldn't go there. It was in the same, forbidden territory that housed flirting and he had never been tempted to respond to opportunities that were only becoming more blatant as time crept on.

No. He couldn't go there. It would still feel like he was being unfaithful…

Nobody could ever accuse Charles Davenport of being less than totally loyal. To his family and to his work.

And that was exactly where his entire focus had to be right now. It didn't matter a damn that this was a less than ideal welcome to a new staff member. Grace would have to jump into the deep end and do her bit to get Manhattan Mercy's ER through this unexpected crisis.

Just as he was doing.

Other staff members were already in the area assigned to deal with major trauma, preparing it for the accident victims they had been warned were on their way. A nurse handed Grace a gown to cover her scrubs and then a face mask that had the plastic eye shield attached.

'Gloves are on the wall there. Choose your size.'

Someone helpfully shone a torch beam over the bench at the side of the area so that Grace could see the 'M' for medium on the front of the box she needed. She also caught a glimpse of an airway cart ready for business, an IV cart, a cardiac monitor, ventilator and portable ultrasound machine.

Okay. She could work with this. Even in semi-darkness she had what she needed to assess an airway, breathing and circulation and to do her best to handle whatever emergencies needed to be treated to stabilise a critically injured patient. And she wasn't alone. As the shadowy figures of paramedics surrounding a gurney came rapidly towards them, Charles was already standing at the head of the bed, ready to take on the most important role of managing an airway.

'Male approximately forty years old,' one of the paramedics told them. He was wearing wet weather gear but his hair was soaked and he had to wipe away the water that was still trickling into his eyes. 'Hit by a truck and thrown about thirty feet to land on the hood of an approaching car. GCS of twelve, blood pressure ninety on palp, tachycardic at one-thirty. Major trauma to left arm and leg.'

The man was semi-conscious and clearly in pain. Despite wearing a neck collar and being strapped to a back board, he was trying to move and groaning loudly.

'On my count,' Charles directed. 'One, two…*three*…'

The patient was smoothly transferred to the bed.

'I need light here, please,' Charles said. He leaned close to their patient's head as someone shone a beam of light in his direction. 'Can you hear me?' He seemed to understand the muffled change to the groan coming from beneath an oxygen mask. 'You're in hospital, buddy. We're going to take care of you.'

A nurse was cutting away clothing. Another was wrapping a blood pressure cuff around an arm and a young, resident doctor was swapping the leads from an ambulance monitor to their own. Grace was watching, assessing the injuries that were becoming apparent. A mangled right arm and a huge wound on the left thigh where a snapped femur had probably gone through the skin and then been pulled back again. The heavy blood loss was an immediate priority. She grabbed a wad of dressing material and put it on the wound to apply direct pressure.

'We need to get back out there,' the lead paramedic told them. 'It's gone crazy. Raining cats and dogs and visibility is almost zero.'

'How widespread is the power cut?'

'At least sixteen blocks from what we've heard. Lightning strike on a power station, apparently. Nobody knows how long it's gonna be before it's back on.'

Charles nodded. 'Thanks, guys.' But his attention was on assessing his patient's breathing. He had crouched to put his line of sight just over head level and Grace knew he was watching the rise and fall of the man's chest to see whether it was symmetrical. If it wasn't, it could indicate a collapsed lung or another problem affecting his breathing.

She was also in a direct line for the steady glance and she saw the shift, when Charles was satisfied with chest movement and had taken on board what she was doing to control haemorrhage and his gaze flicked up to meet her own. For a split second, he held the eye contact and there was something in his gaze that made her feel…what? That he had confidence in her abilities? That she was already a part of the team?

That he was pleased to see her again?

Behind that emotional frisson, there was something else, too. An awareness of how different Charles looked. It shouldn't be a surprise. Thirteen years was a very long time and, even then, they had been young people who were products of their very different backgrounds. But everyone had known that Charles Davenport had the perfect life mapped out for him so why did Grace get the fleeting impression that he looked older than she would have expected? That he had lines in his face that suggested a profound weariness. Sadness, even…

'Blood pressure eighty on forty.' The resident looked up at the overhead monitor. 'And heart rate is one-thirty. Oxygen saturation ninety-four percent.'

'Is that bleeding under control, Grace?'

'Almost. I'd like to get a traction splint on asap for definitive control. It's a mid-shaft femoral fracture.'

Another nod from Charles. 'As soon as you've done that, we need a second line in and more fluids running. And I want an abdominal ultrasound as soon as I've intubated. Can someone ring through to Theatre and see what the situation is up there?'

The buzz of activity around the patient picked up pace and the noise level rose so much that Grace barely noticed the arrival of more paramedics and another patient being delivered to the adjoining trauma room, separated only by curtains. Working conditions were difficult, especially when some of the staff members were directed to the new arrival, but they were by no means impossible. Even with the murky half-light when a torch wasn't being directed at the arm she was working on, Grace managed to get a wide-bore IV line inserted and secured, attaching more fluids to try and stabilise this patient's blood pressure.

With the airway and breathing secured by intubation and ventilation, Charles was able to step back and oversee everything else being done here. He could also watch what was happening on the neighbouring bed, as the curtain had been pulled halfway open. As Grace picked up the ultrasound transducer and squeezed some jelly onto her patient's abdomen, she got a glimpse of what was happening next door.

Judging by the spinal board and the neck collar immobilising the Spanish-looking woman, this was the 'fall down stairs' patient they had been alerted to. What was more of a surprise was that Charles was already in position at the head of this new patient. And he looked…fresher, somehow. Younger…?

No… Grace blinked. It wasn't Charles.

And then she remembered. He'd had a twin brother who'd gone to a different medical school. Elijah? And hadn't their father been the chief of emergency services at a prestigious New York hospital?

This hospital. Of course it was.

Waiting for the image to become readable on her screen as she angled the transducer, Grace allowed herself a moment to think about that. The dynasty was clearly continuing with the Davenport family front and centre in Manhattan Mercy's ER. Hadn't there been a younger sister who was expected to go into medicine as well? It wouldn't surprise her if there was yet another Davenport on the staff here. That was how rich and powerful families worked, wasn't it—sticking together to become even more powerful?

A beat of something like resentment appeared. Or was it an old disappointment that she'd been so insignificant compared to the importance of family for Charles? That she'd become instantly invisible the moment that scandal had erupted?

Whatever. It was easy to push aside. Part of a past that had absolutely nothing to do with the present. Or the future.

'We've got free fluid in the abdomen and pelvis,' she announced. 'Looks like it's coming from the spleen.'

'Let's get him to Theatre,' Charles ordered. 'They've got power and they've been cleared to only take emergencies. He's stable enough for transfer but he needs a medical escort. Grace, can you go with him, please?'

The metallic sounds of brakes being released and sidebars being raised and locked were almost instant. Grace only had time to ensure that IV lines were safe from snagging before the bed began moving. This was an efficient team who were well used to working together and following the directions of their chief. Even in the thick of what had to be an unusually stressful shift for this department, Grace could feel the respect with which Charles was regarded.

Behind her, as she stayed close to the head of the bed to monitor her patient's airway and breathing en route to Theatre, Grace could hear Charles moving onto a new task without missing a beat.

'Any signs of spinal injury, Elijah? Want me to see if the CT lab is clear?'

And then she heard his voice change. 'Oh, my God… *Maria?*'

He must know this patient, she realised. And he was clearly horrified. She could still hear him even though she was some distance on the other side of the curtain now.

'What happened? Where are the boys?'

A break from the barely controlled chaos in a badly lit emergency department was exactly what Grace needed to catch her breath but it was a worry how crowded the corridors were. And a glimpse into the main waiting area as they rushed past on their way to the only elevators being run on a generator suggested that the workload wasn't going to diminish any time soon.

This was a different planet from the kind of environment Grace had been working in for the last few years and the overall impression was initially overwhelming. Why on earth had she thought she could thrive with a volume of work that was so fast-paced? In a totally new place and in a huge city that was at the opposite end of the spectrum from where she'd chosen to be for such a long time.

Because her friend Helena had convinced her that it was time to reconnect with the real world? Because she had become exhausted by relying solely on personal resources to fight every battle that presented itself? Because the isolation of the places she had chosen to practise medicine had finally tipped the balance from being a welcome escape to a bone-deep loneliness that couldn't be ignored for ever?

Like another omen, lights flickered overhead as neon strips came alive with a renewed supply of power. Everybody, including the porters and nurses guiding this bed towards Theatre, looked up and Grace could hear a collective sigh of relief. Normal life would be resumed as soon as the aftermath of this unexpected challenge was dealt with.

And she could cope, too. Possibly even thrive, which had been the plan when she'd signed the contract to begin work in Manhattan Mercy's ER. This was a new beginning and Grace knew better than most that to get the best out of new beginnings you had to draw a line under the past and move on. And yes...

some things needed more time to heal but she had taken that time. A lot more time than she had anticipated needing, in fact.

She was ready.

Having stayed longer than the rest of the transfer team so that she could give the anaesthetist and surgeons a comprehensive handover, Grace found that she needed to find her own way back to the ER and it turned out to be a slightly more circuitous route than before. Instead of passing the main reception area, she went past an orthopaedic room where casts were being applied, what looked like a small operating theatre that was labelled for minor surgery and seemed to have someone having a major laceration stitched and then a couple of smaller rooms that looked as if they had been designed for privacy. Were these rooms used for family consultations, perhaps? Or a space where people could be with a loved one who was dying?

A nurse was peering out of one of the doors.

'Oh, thank goodness,' she said, when she saw Grace approaching. 'I'm about to *burst*… Could you please, please stay with the boys in here for two minutes while I dash to the bathroom?'

The young nurse, whose name badge introduced her as 'Jackie', certainly looked desperate. Having had to grab a bathroom stop herself on her way back from Theatre, Grace could sympathise with the urgency. She was probably already later in her return to the ER than might have been expected so another minute or two wouldn't make any difference, would it?

'Sure,' she said. 'But be as quick as you can?'

Jackie sped off with a grateful smile and vigorous nod without giving Grace the chance to ask anything else—like why these 'boys' were in a side room and whether they needed any medical management.

She turned to go through the door and then froze.

Two small faces were filling the space. Identical faces.

These two children had to be the most adorable little boys she had ever seen. They were about three years old, with tousled mops of dark hair, huge curious eyes and small button noses.

There was something about twins...

For someone who'd had to let go of the dream of even having a single baby, the magic of twins could pack a punch that left a very physical ache somewhere deep inside Grace.

Maybe she wasn't as ready as she'd thought she was to step back into the real world and a new future…

or twine could pack a punch that I'd, a very
physical area somewhere deep inside Grace
Maybe he wasn't as ready as she'd thought
she was to explode, and they'd wait and
new future.

CHAPTER TWO

'WHO ARE YOU?'

'I'm Grace. I'm one of the doctors here.'

It wasn't as hard as she'd expected to find a
smile. Who wouldn't smile at this pair? 'Who
are *you*?'

'I'm Cameron,' one of the boys told her.
'And he's Max.'

'Hello, Max,' Grace said. 'Hello, Cameron.
Can I come into your room?'

'Why?' Cameron seemed to be the spokes-
man for the pair. 'Where's Jackie gone?'

'Just to the bathroom. She'll be back in a
minute. She asked me to look after you.'

'Oh… 'Kay…'

Grace stepped into the room as the children
turned. There was a couch and two armchairs
in here, some magazines on a low table and a
box of toys that had been emptied.

'Are you waiting for somebody?' Grace asked, perching on the arm of the couch.

'Yes. Daddy.' Cameron dropped to his knees and picked up a toy. His brother sat on the floor beside him. 'Here...you can have the fire truck, Max. I'm going to have the p'lice car, 'kay?'

Max nodded. But as he took hold of the plastic fire truck that had been generously gifted with both hands, the back wheels came off.

'Oh...no...' Cameron sounded horrified. 'You *broke* it.'

Max's bottom lip quivered. Grace slid off the arm of the couch and crouched down beside him.

'Let me have a look. I don't think it's very broken. See...?' She clipped the axle of the wheels back into place. 'All fixed.'

She handed the truck back with a smile and, unexpectedly, received a smile back. A delicious curve of a wide little mouth that curled itself instantly right around her heart.

Wow...

'Fank you,' Max said gravely.

'You're so welcome.' Grace's response came out in no more than a whisper.

Love at first sight could catch you unawares in all sorts of different ways, couldn't it? It could be a potential partner for life, or a gorgeous place like a peaceful forest, or a special house or cute puppy. Or it could be a small boy with a heartbreaking smile.

Cameron was pushing his police car across the top of the coffee table and making muted siren noises but Max stayed where he was, with the mended fire truck in his arms. Or not quite where he was. He leaned, so that his head and shoulder were pressed against Grace's arm. It was impossible not to return this gesture of acceptance and it was purely instinctive to shift her arm so that it slid around the small body and let him snuggle more comfortably.

It would only be for a moment because Nurse Jackie would be back any second. Grace could hear people in the corridor outside. She could feel the draught of air as the door was pushed open behind her so she closed her eyes for a heartbeat to help her lock this exquisite fraction of time into her memory banks. This feeling of connection with a precious small person...

'Daddy...' Cameron's face split into a huge grin.

Max wriggled out from under Grace's arm, dropping the fire truck in his haste to get to his feet, but Grace was still sitting on the floor as she turned her head. And then astonishment stopped her moving at all.

'Charles?'

'Grace...' He sounded as surprised as she had. 'What on earth are you doing in here?'

She felt as guilty as a child caught with her hand in a forbidden cookie jar. 'It was only for a minute. To help out...'

'Jackie had to go to the bathroom.' Cameron had hold of one of his father's hands and he was bouncing up and down.

'She fixed the truck,' Max added, clearly impressed with the skills Grace had demonstrated. 'The wheels came off.'

'Oh...' Charles scooped Cameron up with one arm. Max was next and the ease with which two small boys were positioned on each hip with their arms wrapped around their father's neck suggested that this was a very well-practised manoeuvre. 'That's all right, then...'

Charles was smiling, first at one twin and then the other, and Grace felt her heart melt a little more.

She could feel the intense bond between this man and his children. The power of an infinite amount of love.

She'd been wrong about that moment of

doubt earlier, hadn't she? Charles *did* have the perfect life.

'Can we go home now? Is Maria all better?'

Grace was on her feet now. She should excuse herself and get back to where she was supposed to be but something made her hesitate. To stand there and stare at Charles as she remembered hearing the concern in his voice when he'd recognised the new patient in ER.

He was shaking his head now. 'Maria's got a sore back after falling down the stairs. She's going to be fine but she needs to have a rest for a few days.'

He looked up, as if he could feel the questions buzzing in Grace's head.

'Maria is the boys' nanny,' he said. 'I'll be taking a few days' leave to look after them until she's back on her feet. Fortunately, it was only a sprain and not a fracture.'

That didn't stop the questions but Grace couldn't ask why the head of her new department would automatically take time away to care for his children. Where was their mother? Maybe she was another high-achieving medic who was away—presenting at some international conference or something?

Whatever. It was none of her business. And anyway, Jackie the nurse had come back and there was no reason for her to take any more time away from the job she was employed to be doing.

'I'd better get back,' she said. 'Do you still want me to cover Trauma One?'

'Thanks.' Charles nodded. 'I'll come with you. Jackie, I just came to give you some money. The cafeteria should be up and running again now and I thought you could take the boys up for some lunch.'

Planting a kiss on each small, dark head, he deposited the twins back on the floor.

'Be good,' he instructed. 'And if it's not still raining when we go home, we'll stop in the park for a swing.'

He led Grace back towards the main area of the ER.

'It's still crazy in here,' he said. 'But we've got extra staff and it's under control now that we've got power back on.'

'I'm sorry I took so long. I probably shouldn't have stopped to help Jackie out.'

'It's not a problem.'

'They're gorgeous children,' Grace added. 'You're a very lucky man, Charles.'

The look he gave her was almost astonished. Then a wash of something poignant crossed his face and he smiled.

A slow kind of smile that took her back through time instantly. To when the brilliant young man who'd been like royalty in their year at med school had suddenly been interested in her as more than the only barrier he had to be a star academically and not just socially. He had cared about what she had to say. About who she was…

'Yes,' he said slowly. 'I am.'

He held open one of the double doors in front of them. 'How 'bout you, Grace? You got kids?'

She shook her head.

'Too busy with that exciting career I was reading about in your CV? Working with the flying doctors in the remotest parts of the outback?'

Her throat felt tight. 'Something like that.'

She could feel his gaze on her back. A beat of silence—curiosity, even, as if he knew there was a lot being left unspoken.

And then he caught up with her in a single, long stride. Turned his head and, yes… she could see the flicker of curiosity.

'It's been a long time, Grace.'

'It has.'

'Be nice to catch up sometime…'

People were coming towards them. There

were obviously matters that required the attention of the chief and Grace had her own work to do. She could see paramedics and junior staff clustered around a new gurney in Trauma One but she took a moment before she broke that eye contact.

A moment when she remembered that smile from a few moments ago. And so much more, from a very long time ago.

'Yes,' she said quietly. 'It would…'

The rest of that first shift in Manhattan Mercy's emergency department passed in something of a blur for Grace. Trauma related to the storm and power outage continued to roll in. A kitchen worker had been badly burned when a huge pot of soup had been tipped over in the confusion of a crowded restaurant kitchen plunged into darkness. A man had suffered a heart attack while trapped in an elevator and had been close to the end of the time window for curtailing the damage to his cardiac muscle by the time he'd been rescued. A pedestrian had been badly injured when they'd made a dash to get across a busy road in the pouring rain and a woman who relied on her home oxygen supply had been brought to the

ER in severe respiratory distress after it had
been cut off.

Grace was completely focused on each patient that spent time in Trauma One but Charles
seemed to be everywhere, suddenly appearing
where and when he was most needed. How did
he do that?

Sometimes it had to be obvious, of course.
Like when the young kitchen worker arrived
and his screams from the pain of his severe
burns would have been heard all over the
department and the general level of tension
rocketed skywards. He was so distressed he
was in danger of injuring himself further by
fighting off staff as they attempted to restrain
him enough to gain IV access and adminis-
ter adequate pain relief and Grace was almost
knocked off her feet by a flying fist that caught
her hip.

It was Charles who was suddenly there to
steady her before she fell. Charles who positioned security personnel to restrain their
patient safely. And it was Charles who spoke
calmly enough to capture a terrified youth's
attention and stop the agonised cries for long
enough for him to hear what was being said.

'We're going to help you,' he said. 'Try and

hold still for just a minute. It will stop hurting very soon…'

He stayed where he was and took over the task of sedating and intubating the young man. Like everyone else in the department, Grace breathed a sigh of relief as the terrible sounds of agony were silenced. She could assess this patient properly now, start dressing the burns that covered the lower half of his body and arrange his transfer to the specialist unit that could take over his care.

She heard Charles on the phone as she passed the unit desk later, clearly making arrangements for a patient who'd been under someone else's initial care.

'It's a full thickness inferior infarct. He's been trapped in an elevator for at least four hours. I'm sending him up to the catheter laboratory, stat.'

The hours passed swiftly and it was Charles who reminded Grace that it was time she went home.

'We're under control and the new shift is taking over. Go home and have a well-deserved rest, Grace. And thanks,' he added, as he turned away. 'I knew you would be an asset to this department.'

The smile was a reward for an extraordi-

narily testing first day and the words of praise
stayed with Grace as she made her way to the
locker room to find her coat to throw on over
her scrubs.

There were new arrivals in the space, lock-
ing away their personal belongings before they
started their shift. And one of them was a familiar face.

Helena Tate was scraping auburn curls back
from her face to restrain with a scrunchie but
she abandoned the task as she caught sight of
Grace.

'I hear you've had quite a day.'

Grace simply nodded.

'Do you hate me—for persuading you to
come back?'

She shook her head now. 'It's been full on,'
she said, 'but you know what?'

'What?'

Grace felt her mouth curving into a grin. 'I
loved it.'

It was true, she realised. The pace of the
work had left no time for first day nerves. She
had done her job well enough to earn praise
from the chief and, best of all, the moment
she'd been dreading—seeing Charles again—
had somehow morphed into something that
had nothing to do with heartbreak or embar-

rassment or even resentment. It almost felt like a reconnection with an old friend. With a part of her life that had been so full of promise because she'd had no idea of just how tough life could become.

'Really?' Helena let out a huff of relief. 'Oh, I'm so happy to hear that.' She was smiling now. 'So it wasn't weird, finding that someone you went to med school with is your boss now?'

Grace had never confessed the real reason it was going to be awkward seeing Charles Davenport again. She had never told anybody about that night, not even her best friend. And certainly not the man she had married. It had been a secret—a shameful one when it had become apparent that Charles had no desire to remember it.

But today it seemed that she had finally been able to move past something that had been a mere blip of time in a now distant past life.

'Not really,' she told Helena. 'Not that we had time to chat. I did meet his little boys, though.'

'The twins? Aren't they cute? Such a tragic story.' Helena lowered her voice. 'Nina was the absolute love of Charles's life and she died minutes after they were born. Amniotic embolism. He'll never get over it...'

Shock made Grace speechless but Helena didn't seem to notice. The hum of voices around them was increasing as more people came in and out of the locker room. Helena glanced up, clearly refocusing on what was around her. She pulled her hair back again and wound the elastic band around her short ponytail. 'I'd better get in there. You can tell me all about it in the morning.'

The door of her locker shut with a metallic clang to reveal the figure arriving beside her to open another locker. Charles Davenport glanced sideways as Helena kept talking.

'Have my bed tonight,' she told Grace. 'I'll be home so late, a couple of hours on that awful couch won't make any difference.'

And then she was gone. Grace immediately turned to look for her own locker because she didn't want to catch Charles's gaze and possibly reveal that she had just learned something very personal about his life. She turned back just as swiftly, however, as she heard him speak.

'You're sleeping on a couch?'

'Only until I find my own place.' Grace could see those new lines on his face in a different light now and it made something tighten in her chest. He'd suffered, hadn't he?

She knew what that was like...

'It's a bit of a squash,' she added hurriedly. 'But Helena's an old friend. Do you remember her from Harvard?'

Charles shook his head and Grace nodded a beat later. Why would he remember someone who was not only several years younger but, like her, had not been anywhere near the kind of elite social circles the Davenports belonged to? Her own close friendship with Helena had only come about because they'd lived in the same student accommodation block.

'She was a few years behind us. We've kept in touch, though. It was Helena who persuaded me to apply for the job here.'

Charles took a warm coat from its hanger and draped it over his arm. 'I'll have to remember to thank her for that.' He pulled a worn-looking leather satchel from his locker before pushing the door shut. He looked like a man in a hurry. 'I'd better go and rescue my boys. Good luck with the apartment hunting.'

'Thanks. I might need it. From what I've heard, it's a bit of a mission to find something affordable within easy commuting of Central Manhattan.'

'Hmm.' Charles turned away, the sound no more than a sympathetic grunt. But then his head turned swiftly, his eyes narrowed, as if he'd just thought of something important. 'Do you like dogs?'

The random question took Grace by surprise. She blinked at Charles.

'Sorry?'

He shook his head. 'It's just a thought. Might come to nothing but...' He was pulling a mobile phone from the pocket of his scrubs and then tapping on the screen. 'Give me your phone number,' he said. 'Just in case...'

What had he been thinking?

Was he really intending to follow through with that crazy idea that had occurred to him when he'd heard that the newest member of his department was camping in another colleague's apartment and sleeping on an apparently uncomfortable couch?

Why would he do that when his life had suddenly become even more complicated than it already was?

'It's not raining, Daddy.' Zipped up inside his bright red puffer jacket, with a matching woolly hat covering his curls, Cameron tugged on his father's hand. 'Swing?'

Max's tired little face lit up at the reminder and he nodded with enthusiasm. 'I want a swing, too.'

'But it's pouring, guys.' Charles had to smile down at his sons. 'See? You're just dry because you're under my umbrella.'

A huge, black umbrella. Big enough for all of them to be sheltered as they walked beneath dripping branches of the massive trees lining this edge of Central Park, the pavement plastered with the evidence of the autumnal leaf fall. Past one of the more than twenty playgrounds for children that this amazing space boasted, currently empty of any nannies or parents trying to entertain their young people.

'Aww...'

The weight of two tired small boys suddenly increased as their steps dragged.

'And it's too dark now, anyway,' Charles pointed out. 'We'll go tomorrow. In the daytime. We can do that because it's Sunday and there's no nursery school. And I'm going to be at home to look after you.'

'Why?'

'Because Maria's got a sore back.'

'Because she fell down the stairs?'

'That's right, buddy.'

'It went dark,' Cameron said.

'I was scared,' Max added. 'Maria was *crying…*'

'Horse was barking and barking.'

'Was he?'

'I told Max to sit on the stair,' Cameron said proudly. 'And Mr Jack came to help.'

Jack was the elderly concierge for their apartment block and he'd been there for many years before Charles had bought the penthouse floor. He was almost part of the family now.

And probably more willing to help than his real family would be if he told them about the latest complication in his home life.

No, that wasn't fair. His siblings would do whatever they could but they were all so busy with their own lives and careers. Elijah would have to step up to take his place as Chief of Emergency in the next few days. His sister Penelope was on a much-needed break, although she was probably on some adrenaline-filled adventure that involved climbing a mountain or extreme skiing. The youngest Davenport, Zachary, was back from his latest tour of duty and working at the Navy Academy in Annapolis and his half-sister, Miranda, would try *too* hard, even if it was too much. Protecting his siblings had become second nature to Charles ever since the Davenports' sheltered world had imploded all those years ago.

And his parents? Hugo Davenport had retired as Chief of Emergency to allow Charles to take the position but he'd barely had time for his own children as they were growing up and he would be at a complete loss if he was left with the sole responsibility of boisterous twin almost three-year-olds. It would be sole responsibility, too, because Vanessa had led an almost completely separate life ever since the scandal, and playing happy grandparents together would never be added to her agenda.

His mother would rush to help, of course, and put out the word that she urgently needed the services of the best nanny available in New York but Charles didn't want that. He didn't want a stranger suddenly appearing in his home. His boys had to feel loved and totally secure at all times. He'd promised them that much when they were only an hour old—in those terrible first minutes after their mother's death.

His grip tightened on the hand of each twin.

'You were both very brave in the dark,' he told them. 'And you've both been a big help by being so good when you had to stay at Daddy's work all day. I'm very, very proud of you both.'

'So we can go to the park?'

'Tomorrow,' he promised. 'We'll go to the park even if it's still raining. You can put your rubber boots on and jump in all the puddles.'

They could take some time out and make the outside world unimportant for an hour or two. Maybe he would be able to put aside the guilt that he was taking emergency leave from his work and stop fretting that he was creating extra pressure for Elijah or that his other siblings would worry about him when they heard that he was struggling as a single parent—yet again. Maybe he could even forget about the background tension of being part of a family that was a far cry from the united presence they could still display for the sake of a gala fundraising event or any other glittering, high-society occasion. A family whose motto of 'What happens in the family stays in the family' had been sorely tested but had, in recent years, regained its former strength.

A yellow taxi swooped into the kerb, sending a spray of water onto the pavement. Charles hurried the twins past a taco restaurant, souvenir shop, a hot dog stand and the twenty-four-seven deli to turn into the tree-lined avenue that was the prestigious address for the brownstone apartment block they called home.

And it was then that Charles recognised why he'd felt the urge to reach out and try to help Grace Forbes.

Like taking the boys to the park, it felt like he had the opportunity to shut the rest of the world out to some extent.

Grace was part of a world that had ceased to exist when the trauma of the family trouble had threatened everything the Davenport family held dear. It had been the happiest time of Charles's life. He had been achieving his dream of following in his father's footsteps and becoming a doctor who could one day be in charge of the most challenging and exciting place he had ever known—Manhattan Mercy's ER. The biggest problem he'd had was how to balance a demanding social life with the drive to achieve the honour of topping his class, and the only real barrier to that position had been Grace.

He'd managed to succeed, despite the appalling pressure that had exploded around him in the run-up to final exams, by focusing only on the things that mattered the most—supporting his mother and protecting his siblings from the fallout of scandal and passing those exams with the best possible results. He had been forced to dismiss Grace, along with every other social aspect of his life. And he'd learned to dismiss any emotion that could threaten his goals.

But he had never forgotten how simple and happy his life at medical school had been up until that point.

And, if he was honest, he'd never forgotten that night with Grace...

He could never go back, of course, but the pull of even connecting with it from a distance was surprisingly compelling. And what harm could it do? His life wasn't about to change. He had his boys and he had his job and that was all he needed. All he could ever hope for.

But Grace had been special. And there was something about her that made him think that, perhaps—like him—life hadn't quite turned out the way she'd planned. Or deserved?

'Shall we stop and say hello to Horse before we go upstairs?'

'*Yes*...' The tug on his hands was in a forward direction now, instead of a reluctant weight he was encouraging to follow him. 'Let's *go*, Daddy...'

CHAPTER THREE

'SO HERE'S THE THING…'

'Mmm?' Grace was still trying to get her head around hearing Charles Davenport's voice on a phone for the first time ever.

The twang of a New York accent had probably been mellowed by so many years at exclusive, private schools but his enunciation was crisp. Decisive, even. It made her think of someone in a suit. Presenting a killer summary in a courtroom, perhaps. Or detailing a take-over bid in the boardroom of a global company.

She was sitting cross-legged on the couch in Helena's apartment, a take-out container of pad Thai on her lap and a pair of chopsticks now idle in her hands. She was in her pyjamas already, thanks to getting soaked in the tail end of the storm during her long walk home from the nearest subway station.

Was her attire partly responsible for hearing that slightly gravelly edge to Charles's voice that made her think that he would sound just like that if his head was on a pillow, very close to her own?

'Sorry…did you say your neighbour's name was *Houston*? As in "Houston, we have a problem"?'

The chuckle of laughter came out of the phone and went straight for somewhere deep in Grace's chest. Or maybe her belly. It created a warmth that brought a smile to her face.

'Exactly. It's their dog that's called Houston and they chose the name on the first day they brought him home as a puppy when they found what he'd left in the middle of their white carpet.'

The bubble of her own laughter took Grace by surprise. Because it felt like the kind of easy laughter that she hadn't experienced in such a long time? The kind that made her think of a first date? Or worse, made her remember *that* night. When Charles had found her, so stressed before the start of their final exams that she was in pieces and he'd tried to reassure her. To distract her, by talking to her rather like this. By making her laugh through her tears and then…

And then there'd been that astonishing moment when they couldn't break the eye contact between them and the kiss that had started everything had been as inevitable as the sun rising the next morning.

It was an effort to force herself to focus on what Charles was actually saying as he kept talking.

'The boys call him Horse, because they weren't even two when he arrived and they couldn't pronounce Houston but he's quite big so that seemed to work, too.'

Grace cleared her throat, hoping her voice would come out sounding normal. How embarrassing would it be if it was kind of husky and betrayed those memories that refused to stay where they should be. Buried.

'What sort of dog is he?'

'A retro doodle. Half poodle, half golden retriever. One of those designer, hypo-allergenic kind of dogs, you know? But he's lovely. Very well behaved and gentle.'

Grace closed her eyes for a moment. This was *so* weird. She hadn't seen Charles Davenport in more than a decade but here they were chatting about something completely random as if they were friends who caught up every other week. And they'd never been *friends*,

exactly. Friend*ly*, certainly—with a lot of respect for each other's abilities. And they'd been
passionate—so briefly it had always seemed
like nothing more than a fantasy that had unexpectedly achieved reality. But this?

Thanks to the memories it was stirring up,
this was doing Grace's head in.

On top of that, her noodles were getting cold
and probably wouldn't appreciate another spin
in the microwave.

The beat of an awkward silence made her
wonder if this apparently easy chatting was
actually just as weird for Charles.

'Anyway…I'm sorry to disturb your evening
but it occurred to me that it could be a win-
win situation.'

'Oh?'

'Houston's parents are my neighbours on the
ground floor of this block—which, I should
mention, is about two minutes' walk to Central
Park and ten at the most to Manhattan Mercy.'

'Oh…' How good would that be, not to have
to battle crowds in the subway and a long walk
at the end of the commute?

'Stefan's an interior designer and his husband, Jerome, is an artist. They're heading
off tomorrow for a belated honeymoon in Europe and they'll be gone for about six weeks.

They're both fretting about Houston having to go into kennels. I suggested they get a dog-sitter to live in but...' Charles cleared his throat as if he was slightly embarrassed. 'Apparently Houston is their fur child and they couldn't find someone trustworthy enough. When I got home this evening, I told them about you and they seem to be very impressed with the recommendation I gave them.'

'Oh...?' Good grief, she was beginning to sound like a broken record. 'But...I work long hours. I couldn't look after a dog...'

'Houston has a puppy walker that he loves who would come twice a day on the days that you're working. That's another part of his routine that Stefan and Jerome are worried about disrupting because he gets to play with his dog friends who get taken out at the same time. Even more importantly, if he was still in his own home, he wouldn't miss his dads so much. And I thought that it could give you a bit of breathing space, you know? To find your feet in a new city and where you want to be.'

Not just breathing space. Living space. Sharing a tiny apartment, even with a good friend, was a shock to the system for someone who had guarded their privacy so well for so long.

'I know it's all very last minute with them

being due to drop Houston at the kennels in the morning but they're home this evening and they'd love to meet you and have a chat about it. Stefan said he'd be delighted to cover your taxi fares if you were at all interested.' Charles paused and Grace could hear something that sounded like a weary sigh. 'Anyway...I've only just got the boys to bed and I need to have a hunt in the fridge and see if I can find something to eat that isn't the boys' favourite packet mac and cheese.'

Again, Grace was aware of that tightness in her chest. Empathy? Charles might have the blessing of having two gorgeous children but he had lost something huge as well. Something that had changed his future for ever—the loss of a complete family.

They had a lot more than he realised in common.

Her new boss had also had a very difficult day, coping with a crisis in his department and the added blow of having to deal with a personal crisis with his nanny being put out of action. And yet he'd found the time to think about her and a way to possibly help her adjust to a dauntingly huge change in her life?

How astonishing was that?

'Thank you so much, Charles.' Grace dropped

the chopsticks into the plastic bowl and put it onto the coffee table as she unfurled her legs. It didn't matter that she would have to get dressed again and then head out into this huge city that never slept. Despite so much going on in his own life, Charles had made a very thoughtful effort on her behalf and she knew exactly how she needed to show her appreciation.

There was something else prompting her, too. A niggle that was purely instinctive that was telling her not to miss this unexpected opportunity. That it might, somehow, be a signpost to the new path in life that she was seeking. The kind of niggle that had persuaded her, in the end, to come to New York in the first place.

'Let me grab a pen. Give me the address and I'll get there as soon as I can.'

'Morning, Doc.'

'Morning, Jack. How's the weather looking out there?' Not that Charles needed to ask. The view from his penthouse apartment over Central Park and the Manhattan skyline had shown him that any residual cloudiness from the storm of a few days ago had been blown well clear of the city. It was a perfect October day. But discussing the weather was a ritual. And it gave him the chance to make sure that the twins were well protected from the chill, with their jackets fastened, ears covered by their hats and twenty little fingers encased in warm mittens.

'It's a day for the park, that's fo' sure.' Jack had a passion for following meteorology and spent any free time on door duty surfing weather channels. 'High of sixteen degrees, thirty-two percent clear skies and twenty-one percent chance of light rain but that won't happen until after two p.m.'

'Perfect. Nice change, isn't it?' As usual, Cameron's mittens were hanging by the strings that attached them to his jacket sleeves. Charles pulled them over the small hands. 'That was some storm we had the other day.'

'Sure was. Won't forget that in a hurry. Not with poor Maria crashing down the stairs like that.' Jack shook his head. 'How's she doin'?'

'Good, but I don't want her coming back to work too soon. She won't be up to lifting small boys out of trouble for a while.' Charles tugged Max's hat down over his ears. 'You guys ready?'

'Can we say "hi" to Horse?'

Charles glanced behind the boys, to the door

that led to one of the two ground-floor apartments. He'd been tempted to knock on that door more than once in the last few days—ever since he'd heard the news that Grace had taken on the dog-sitting gig—but something had held him back.

Something odd that felt almost like shyness, which was ridiculous because hanging back had never been an attribute that anyone would associate with the Davenport family.

Maybe he was just waiting for it to happen naturally so that it didn't seem like he was being pushy? He was her boss, after all. Or he would be, as soon as he got back to work properly. There were boundaries here and maybe Grace didn't want to cross them, either. That might explain why she hadn't knocked on *his* door.

He turned, holding out his hands. 'Let's go. Or you'll be wanting a hotdog before we even get to the playground.'

Jack was holding open the front door, letting sunlight stream in to brighten the mosaic tiles of the entrance foyer, but the boys weren't moving to take their father's hands. They were going in the opposite direction, as the door behind Charles swung open.

'Horse...'

The big woolly dog looked as pleased to see the twins as they were to see him. He stood there with what looked like a grin on his face, the long plume of his tail waving, as Cameron and Max wrapped their arms around his neck and buried their faces in his curls.

Grace was grinning as well, as she looked down at the reunion.

'Oh, yeah…cuddles are the best way to start the day, aren't they, Houston?'

She was still smiling as she looked up. The black woollen hat she was wearing made a frame that seemed to accentuate the brightness of that smile. A smile that went all the way to her eyes and made them sparkle.

'We're off to the park,' she said. 'It's my first day off so I'm on dog-walking duty today.'

'We're going to the park, too,' Cameron shouted. 'You can come with us.'

'I want to throw the ball for Horse.' Max nodded.

'I think he has to stay on his lead,' Grace said. 'I've been reading the rules this morning.'

Charles nodded. 'And he's not allowed in the playgrounds. But we can walk with him for a while.'

Grace's smile seemed to wobble, as if a shadow was crossing her face, and Charles had the impression that this was a bigger deal than he would have expected.

'If Grace doesn't mind the extra company, that is,' he added.

'I'd love it,' Grace said firmly. She was clipping the dog's lead onto his harness so Charles couldn't see if she really meant that but then she straightened and caught his gaze.

'You can show me the best places to walk. I don't know anything about Central Park.'

Her smile was strong again and he could see a gleam in her eyes that he remembered very well. He'd seen it often enough in the past, usually when they were both heading in to the same examination.

Determination, that was what it was.

But why did she need to tap into that kind of reserve for something that should be no problem? A pleasure, even...

It was puzzling.

'Have you never been to New York before?' Juggling two small children and a dog on the busy pavement meant that Charles had to wait until they were almost at the gates of the park to say anything more to Grace.

'Never. I was born in Australia and then my family moved to Florida when my dad got a job with NASA.' She was smiling again. 'He thinks it's hilarious that I've got a job looking after a dog called Houston. Anyway…coming here was always a plan once I got to medical school in Boston but there never seemed to be enough time. I was too busy studying…' The glance Charles received was mischievous. 'Trying to keep up with you.'

'I think it was the other way round.' Charles kept a firm grip on small mittened hands, as he paused to wait until a horse-drawn carriage rolled past, carrying tourists on a relaxed tour of the park, but he was holding Grace's gaze as well. They would have to part company very soon and it felt…disappointing?

'Okay…we have two favourite playgrounds close to here but…'

'But dogs aren't allowed, I know. When I looked on the map, there was a track called the Bridle Path? That sounds like a nice place to walk.'

'It is. Come with us as far as the playground and I'll show you which direction to take to find it. Next time, I'll bring the boys' bikes and we can all go on the Bridle Path.'

The way Grace's eyes widened revealed her surprise, which was quite understandable because Charles was a little surprised himself that the suggestion had emerged so casually.

As if this was already a thing—this walking in the park together like a…like a *family*? A whole family, with two parents and even a dog.

And her surprise quickly morphed into something else. Something softer that hadn't been fuelled by determination. Pleasure, even? Was she enjoying their company as much as he was enjoying hers?

Charles was silent the rest of the way to the playground. Not that anybody seemed to notice because Cameron and Max were making sure that Grace didn't miss any of the important attractions.

'Look, Gace…it's a *sk-wirrel*…'

'Oh, yes…I *love* squirrels.'

'Look at all the leafs. Why are they all on the ground?'

'Because it's autumn. The trees get undressed for winter. Like you do when you're getting ready for bed. Aren't they pretty?'

Why had it felt so natural up until now, Charles wondered, to add feminine and canine company to his little troupe when it could be seen as potentially disturbing? He and his boys didn't need extra people in their lives. Against quite a few odds, he had managed perfectly well up until now and his children were happy and healthy and safe…

At least things would go back to normal any second now. Grace would continue her dog walk and he'd stand around with the other parents, watching the children run and climb and shout, until he was summoned to push the swings.

But when they got to the wrought-iron fence surrounding the playground, it seemed that his boys wanted a larger audience for their exploits.

'I want Horse to watch me on the slide,' Cameron said.

'And Gace,' Max added. His face was serious enough to let them know that this was important. 'Gace can push me on the swing.'

'Um...' Grace hadn't missed the slightly awkward edge to the atmosphere in the last minute or two because it had left her feeling just a bit confused.

She'd been happy to have company on her first walk to Central Park because it was always so much easier to go somewhere new with somebody who knew the way. And because it had been so good to see the twins again. Especially Max. Cameron's smile was identical, of course, but there was something a little more serious about Max that pulled her heartstrings so hard it was too close to pain to be comfortable. That was why, for a heartbeat back at the apartment block, she had wondered if it wasn't a good idea to share even a part of this walk. But she'd pushed aside any deeply personal misgivings. Maybe it did still hurt that she would never be part of her own family group like this, but surely she could embrace this moment for what it was? Being included, instead of watching from a distance?

Having Houston walking by her side helped a lot. In fact, the last few days had been a revelation. Due to her work hours and never settling in one place for very long, Grace had never considered adopting a dog and getting to know Houston had been a joy. She wished she'd learned years ago that a companion like this could make you feel so much less alone in the world.

Charles's company was surprisingly good, too. When she'd told him of her father's amusement about the dog's name, the appreciative glint in his eyes made her remember how easy that telephone conversation the other night had been. How close to the surface laughter had felt. He'd caught her memory of how focused life had been back in medical school, too, but twisted it slightly, to make it sound as if he'd been a lot more aware of her than she had realised.

And then he'd made that comment about them all coming to the park again together, as if this was the start of something that he'd expected to happen all along? That was when the awkwardness had sprouted.

Had he somehow heard the alarm bells sounding in her own head or did he have a warning system of his own?

Maybe she should just say goodbye and head off with Houston to explore the park and leave Charles to have time with his boys.

Except…it felt like it would suddenly be less interesting. A bit lonely, even?

And the way Max was looking up at her, with those big, blue eyes, as if her being here was the most important thing in the world to him. He had eyes just like his father, she realised. That amazingly bright blue, made even more striking by the darker rim around the irises.

'I have to stay here, on this side of the fence. To look after Horse.' She smiled at Max. 'But I could watch Daddy push you?'

Houston seemed perfectly happy to sit by her side and Grace was grateful for the dog's warmth as he leaned against her leg. She watched Charles lift the little boys into the bucket seats of the swings, side by side, and then position himself between them so that he could push a swing with each hand. She could see the huge grins on the children's faces and hear the peals of their laughter as the arc of movement got steadily higher. And Charles finally looked exactly as she'd remembered him. Happy. Carefree. Enjoying all the best things in life that automatically came his way because he was one of life's golden people that always had the best available.

Except she knew better now. Charles might have had a very different upbringing from her solid, middle-class existence, but he hadn't been protected from the hard things in life any more than she had. His world had been shattered, maybe as much as hers had been, but he was making the best of it and clearly fatherhood was just as important to him as his work. More important, perhaps. He hadn't hesitated in taking time off when his children needed him.

That said a lot about who he was, didn't it? About his ability to cherish the things that were most important in life?

A beat of something very poignant washed

through Grace as she remembered those whispered words in the locker room.

'Nina was the absolute love of his life...he'll never get over it...'

The death of his wife was utterly tragic but how lucky had they both been to find a love like that? She certainly hadn't been lucky enough to find it in her marriage and she wasn't about to stumble across it any time soon.

Grace closed her eyes for a heartbeat as she let her breath escape in a sigh. How good was this kind of weather, when she could snuggle beneath layers of warm clothes and a lovely, puffy jacket? Nobody would ever guess what she was hiding.

Charles was smiling again as he came back towards her. He hadn't bothered with a hat or gloves and he was rubbing his hands together against the chill of the late autumn air. The breeze was ruffling his hair, which looked longer and more tousled than Grace remembered. Maybe he didn't get much time for haircuts these days. Or maybe how he looked wasn't a priority. It would be ironic if that was the reason, because the tousled look, along with that designer stubble, actually made him look way more attractive.

'That's my duty done. Now I get to watch them run around and climb things until they either get hungry or need to go to the toilet. Probably both at the same time.'

'I should get going. Horse isn't getting the exercise I promised him.'

'Wait a bit? The boys won't forgive me if you disappear before they've had a chance to show off a bit.'

'Sure.'

With the bars of the fence between them and Charles's attention back on his children, it felt curiously safe to be standing this close to him. It was safe anyway, Grace reminded herself. The last thing Charles Davenport would want would be another complication in his life and nobody could take the place of the twins' mother, anyway. With another wash of that empathy, the words came out before Grace thought to filter them.

'You must miss their mom so much...'

The beat of silence between them was surprisingly loud against the backdrop of happy shrieks and laughter from the small crowd of children swarming over the playground attractions. She couldn't miss the way Charles swallowed so carefully.

'So much,' he agreed. 'I can only be thankful that the boys will never feel that loss.'

Grace was silent but she could feel her brow furrowing as Charles slid a brief glance back in her direction.

'Oh, they'll know that something's missing from their life as they get older and notice that all the other kids have moms but they never knew Nina. She didn't even get to hold them.'

'I'm so sorry, Charles,' Grace said quietly. 'I had no idea until Helena mentioned it the other day. I can't even imagine how awful that must have been.'

'We had no warning.' His voice sounded raw. 'The pregnancy had gone so well and we were both so excited about welcoming the twins. Twins run in the family, you know. My brother Elijah is my twin. And we knew they were boys.'

Grace was listening but didn't say anything. She couldn't say anything because her treacherous mind was racing down its own, private track. Picking the scab off an old, emotional wound. Imagining what it would be like to have an enormous belly sheltering not one but *two* babies. She could actually feel a wash of that excitement of waiting for the birth.

'The birth was textbook perfect, too. Cameron arrived and then five minutes later Max did. They were a few weeks early but healthy enough not to need any intervention. I had just cut Max's umbilical cord and was lifting him up to put him in Nina's arms when it happened. She suddenly started gasping for breath and her blood pressure crashed. She was unconscious even before the massive haemorrhage started.'

'Oh… *God*…' Grace wasn't distracted by any personal baggage now. She was in that room with Charles and his two newborn sons. Watching his wife die right in front of his eyes. Her own eyes filled with tears.

'Sorry…' Charles sucked in a deep breath. 'It's not something I ever talk about. I feel… guilty, you know?'

'What? How could you possibly feel *guilty*? There was nothing you could have done.'

'There *should* have been.' There was an intensity to his voice that made the weight of the burden Charles carried very clear. 'It was my job to protect her. I was a doctor, for God's sake. I should have seen something. Some warning. She could have had a medically controlled birth. A Caesarean.'

'It could still have happened.' Grace could hear an odd intensity in her own voice now.

Why did it seem so important to try and convince Charles that he had nothing to feel guilty about? 'A C-section might not have made any difference. These things are rare but they happen—with no warning. Sometimes, you lose the babies as well.' She glanced away from Charles, her gaze drawn to the two happy, healthy little boys running around in the playground. 'Look at them,' she said softly. 'Feel blessed...not guilty...'

Charles nodded. 'I do. Those boys are the most important thing in my life. They *are* my life. It's just that it gets harder at this time of year. It sucks that the anniversary of losing Nina is also the twins' birthday. They're old enough to know about birthdays now and that they're supposed to be happy. And it's Halloween, for heaven's sake. Every kid in the country is getting dressed up and having fun.'

'That's next week.'

'Yeah.' Charles pushed his fingers through his hair as he watched Max follow Cameron through a tunnel at the base of the wooden fort. 'And, thanks to their little friends at nursery school, they're determined to go trick or treating for the first time. And they all wear their costumes to school that day.'

Clearly, it was the last thing Charles wanted to think about. The urge to offer help of some kind was powerful but that might not be something Charles wanted, either. But, he'd opened up to her about the tragedy, hadn't he? And he'd said that he never talked about it but he'd told her. Oddly, that felt remarkably special.

Grace bit her lip, absently scratching Houston's ear as he leaned his head against her leg.

'I wonder if they do Halloween costumes for dogs,' she murmured.

Clearly, Charles picked up on this subtle offer to help make this time of year more fun. More of a celebration than a source of painful memories. His startled glance reminded her of the one she'd received the other day when she'd told him what a lucky man he was to have such gorgeous children. As if he was unexpectedly looking at something from a very different perspective.

If so, he obviously needed time to think about it and that was fine by Grace. Maybe she did, too. Offering to help—to become more involved in this little family—might very well be a mistake. So why did it feel so much like the right thing to do?

Charles was watching the boys again as they

emerged from the other end of the tunnel and immediately ran back to do it all over again.

'Enough about me,' he said. 'I was trying to remember the last time I heard about you and it was at a conference about ten years ago. I'm sure someone told me that you'd got married.'

'Mmm.'

Charles was leaning against the wrought-iron rails between them, so that when he turned his head, he seemed very close. 'But you're not married now?'

'No.'

He held her gaze. He'd just told her about the huge thing that had changed his life for ever. He wasn't going to ask any more questions but he wanted to know her story, didn't he?

He'd just told her about his personal catastrophe that he never normally told anyone. She *wanted* to tell him about hers. To tell him everything. To reveal that they had a connection in grief that others could never understand completely.

But it was the recognition of that connection that prevented her saying anything. Because it was a time warp. She was suddenly back in that blip of time that had connected them that first time. Outside, on a night that had been almost cold enough to freeze her tears.

She could hear his voice.

'Grace? Oh, my God...are you crying? What's wrong?'

He hadn't asked any more questions then, either. He'd known that it didn't actually matter what had gone wrong, it was comfort that she'd needed. Reassurance.

'Come with me. It's far too cold to be out here...'

He could see that there was something huge that had gone wrong now, too. And maybe she wouldn't need to say anything. If that rail wasn't between them, maybe Charles would take her in his arms again.

The way he had that night, before he'd led her away to a warm place.

His room.

His bed.

It was a very good thing that that strong rail was there. That Charles couldn't come through the gate when he had to be in that playground to supervise his children.

Even though she knew it couldn't happen, Grace still pulled her layers of protective clothing a little more tightly around her body. She still found herself stepping back from the fence.

'I really should go,' she said. 'It's not fair to make Houston wait any longer for his walk.'

Charles nodded slowly. His smile said it was fine.

But his eyes told her that he knew she was running away. That he could see a lot more than she wanted him to.

He couldn't see the physical scars, of course. Nobody got to see those.

Grace had been confident that nobody could see the emotional scars, either.

Until now...

CHAPTER FOUR

IT MIGHT WELL have been the two cops standing outside a curtained cubicle that attracted his attention as he walked past.

If he'd had any inclination to analyse it, though, Charles would probably have realised that it was the voice on the other side of the curtain that made him slow down.

Grace's voice.

'Looks like we've got an entrance wound here. And...an exit wound here. But it's possible that they're two entrance wounds. We need an X-ray.'

One of the cops caught his gaze and responded to the raised eyebrow.

'Drive-by shooting,' he said. 'He's lucky. It was his arm and not his head.'

With a nod, Charles moved on. Grace clearly had things under control. She always did, whenever he noticed her in the department and that was almost every day now that he had adjusted his hours to fit around nursery school for the twins. More than once a day, too. Not that he went out of his way to make their paths cross or anything. It just seemed to happen.

Okay, maybe he was choosing to do some necessary paperwork at one side of the unit desk instead of tucked away in his office but that was because he liked to keep half an eye on how the whole department was functioning. He could see the steady movement of people and equipment and hear phone calls being made and the radio link to the ambulance service. If anybody needed urgent assistance, he could be on his feet and moving in an instant.

It had nothing to do with the fact that Grace would be in this area before too long, checking the X-rays that would arrive digitally on one of the bank of departmental computer screens beside him.

He had a sheaf of statistics that he needed to review, like the numbers and types of patients that were coming through his department and it was important to see how they stacked up and whether trends were changing. Level one patients were the critical cases that took the most in the way of personnel and resources, but too many level four or five patients could create barriers to meeting target times for treatment and patient flow.

Grace Forbes certainly wasn't wasting time with her patients. It was only minutes later that she was logging in to a computer nearby, flanked by two medical students and a junior doctor. As they waited to upload files, she glanced sideways and acknowledged Charles with a smile but then she peered intently at the screen. Her colleagues leaned in as she used the cursor to highlight what she was looking at.

'There... Can you see that?'

'Is it a bone fragment?'

'No. Look how smooth the edges of the humerus are. And this is well away from it.'

'So it's a bullet fragment?'

'Yes. A very small one.'

'Do we need to get it out?'

'No. It's not clinically significant. And we were right that it's only one entrance and an exit wound but it was also right to check.'

'Want me to clean and dress it, then?' The junior doctor was keen to take over the case. 'Let the cops take him in to talk to him?'

'Yes. We'll put him on a broad-spectrum antibiotic as well. And make sure he gets a tetanus shot. Thanks, Danny. You're in charge now.' Grace's attention was swiftly diverted as she saw an incoming stretcher and she straightened and moved smoothly towards the new arrival as if she'd been ready and waiting all along.

'Hi, honey.' The girl on the stretcher looked very young, very pale and very frightened. 'My name's Grace and I'm going to be looking after you.'

Charles could hear one of the paramedics talking to Grace as they moved past to a vacant cubicle.

'Looks like gastro. Fever of thirty-nine point five and history of vomiting and diarrhoea. Mom called us when she fainted.'

'BP?'

'Eighty systolic. Couldn't get a diastolic.'

'I'm not surprised she fainted, then…'

The voices faded but Charles found himself still watching, even after the curtain had twitched into place to protect the new patient's privacy.

His attention was well and truly caught this time.

Because he was puzzled.

At moments like this, Grace was exactly the person he would have predicted that she would become. Totally on top of her work. Clever, competent and confident. She got along well with all her colleagues, too. Charles had heard more than one report of how great she was to work with and how generous she was with her time for staff members who were here to learn.

Thanks to the challenge that had been thrown at her within the first minutes of her coming to work here, Charles already knew how good Grace was at her job and how well she coped with difficult circumstances. That ability to think on her feet and adapt was a huge advantage for someone who worked in Emergency and she demonstrated the same kind of attitude in her private life, too, didn't she—in the way she had jumped on board, under pressure, to take on the dog-sitting offer.

But...and this was what was puzzling Charles so much...there was something very different about her personality away from work.

Something that felt off-key.

A timidity, almost. Lack of confidence, anyway.

Vulnerability? The way she'd shrunk away from him at the park yesterday. When he'd ventured onto personal ground by asking her about her marriage. He'd been puzzled then and he hadn't been able to shake it off.

He didn't want to shake it off, in fact. It was

quite nice having this distraction because it meant he could ignore the background tension he always had at this time of year when he was walking an emotional tightrope between celebrating the joy of the twins' birth and being swamped by the grief of losing Nina, which was a can of mental worms that included so many other things he felt he should have done better—like protecting his family during the time of that scandal.

A nurse appeared from behind the curtain, with a handful of glass tubes full of blood that were clearly being rushed off for testing. He caught a glimpse of Grace bent over her patient, with her stethoscope in her ears and a frown of concentration on her face.

Grace had understood that grief so easily. He could still see those tears shimmering in her eyes when she'd been listening to him. Perhaps he'd known that she would understand on a different level from anybody else and that was why he had chosen to say more to her than he would have even to members of his own family.

But how had he known that?

And why was it that she did understand so clearly?

Who had she lost? Her husband, obviously,

but the tone of her limited response to his que-
ries had made him think that it was a marriage
that simply hadn't worked out, not one that had
been blown apart by tragedy, as his had been.

He wanted to know, dammit.

More than that, and he knew that it was ridiculous, but he was a bit hurt by being shut
out.

Why?

Because—once upon a time—she had fallen
into his arms and told him everything she was
so worried about? That the pressure of those
final exams was doing her head in? That it
was times like this that she felt so lonely because it made her miss the mother she'd lost
more than ever?

He'd had no intention of revisiting the memories of that night but they were creeping back
now. The events that threatened to derail his
life that had crashed around him so soon after
that night had made it inevitable that it had to
be dismissed but there was one aspect he'd
never completely buried.

That sense of connection with another person.

He'd never felt it before that night.

He'd been lucky enough to find it again—
with Nina—but he'd known that any chance

of a third strike was out of the question. He wasn't looking because he didn't want to find it.

But it was already there with Grace, wasn't it? It had been, from the moment he'd taken her into his arms that night to comfort her.

And he'd felt it again at the park, when he'd seen her crying for his loss.

She'd been crying that night, too…

'You okay?'

'Huh?' Charles blinked as he heard the voice beside him. 'I'm fine, thanks, Miranda.'

'Okay…' But his half-sister was frowning at him. 'It's not like you to be sitting staring into space.'

Her frown advertised concern. A closeness that gave Charles a beat of something warm. Something good. Because it had been hard won? Miranda had come into their family as a penniless, lonely and frightened sixteen-year-old who was desperately missing her mother who had just died. It had been Charles who'd taken on the responsibility of trying to make her feel wanted. A little less lonely. Trying to persuade her that the scandal hadn't been *her* fault.

'I was just thinking.' About Grace. And he needed to stop because he was still aware of that warmth of something that felt good but now it was coming from remembering something Grace had said. The way she had tried to convince him that he had no valid reason to feel guilty over Nina's death—as if she really cared about how he felt.

Charles tapped the pile of papers in front of him. 'I'm up to my eyeballs in statistics. What are you up to?'

'I need a portable ultrasound to check a stab wound for underlying damage. It looks superficial but I want to make absolutely sure.' Miranda looked around. 'They seem to have gone walkabout.'

Charles glanced towards the glass board where patient details were constantly updated to keep track of where people were and what was going on. Who could be currently using ultrasound to help a diagnosis?

'It could be in with the abdo pain in Curtain Two.'

'Thanks. I'll check.' Miranda turned her head as she moved away. 'How are the party plans going? Do we get an invitation this year?'

Charles shook his head but offered an apologetic smile. 'I'm keeping it low-key. I'm taking them to visit the grandparents the next day for afternoon tea and I'm sure you'll be invited as well, but my neighbours have said they'd be delighted to have an in-house trick or treat happen on the actual birthday and that's probably as much excitement as two three-year-olds can handle.'

Miranda's nod conveyed understanding of the need to keep the celebration private. She'd seen photographs of the Davenport extravaganzas of years past, before she'd become a part of the family—when there had been bouncy castles, magicians and even ponies or small zoos involved.

Buying into Halloween was a big step forward this year but there was going to be a nursery school parade so the costumes were essential. Charles found himself staring again at the curtain that Grace was behind. Hadn't she said something about finding a costume for Houston? Maybe she'd found a good costume shop.

And maybe Houston could join in the fun? The boys loved that dog and he could be an addition to the private party that would delight them rather than overwhelm them, like a full-on Davenport gathering had the potential to do.

Grace would have to be invited, too, of course, but that wasn't a big deal. Somehow, the intrigue about what had happened to change her had overridden any internal warning about spending time with her. He wanted an answer to the puzzle and getting a little closer was the only way he was going to solve the mystery. Close enough to be friends—like he and Miranda had become all those years ago—but nothing more. And that wouldn't be a problem. The barrier to anything more was so solid he wouldn't have the first idea how to get past it.

And he didn't want to. Even the reminder that that barrier was there was enough to send him back to safe territory and Charles spent the next fifteen minutes focused on the graphs he needed to analyse.

But then Grace appeared from the cubicle and headed straight to the computer closest to where he was sitting. It was tempting to say something totally inappropriate, like asking her whether she might be available for a while in two days' time, to go trick or treating but this wasn't the time or place. It was a bit of a shock, in fact, that the urge was even there. So out of character that it wasn't at all difficult to squash.

'Looking for results?'

'Yep. White blood count and creatinine

should be available by now. I've got cultures, throat swabs and urine pending.'

'More than a viral illness, then?'

Grace didn't seem surprised that he was aware of which patient she was dealing with.

'I think she's got staphylococcal toxic shock syndrome. Sixteen years old.'

Charles blinked. It was a rare thing to see these days, which meant that it could be missed until it was late enough for the condition to be extremely serious.

'Signs and symptoms?'

'High fever, vomiting and diarrhoea, muscle aches, a widespread rash that looks like sunburn. She's also hypotensive. Seventy-five over thirty and she's onto her second litre of fluid resus.' Grace flicked him a glance. 'She also finished her period two days ago and likes to leave her tampons in overnight.'

Charles could feel his mouth twisting into a lopsided smile. An impressed one. That was the key question that needed to be asked and could be missed. But not by Grace Forbes, apparently.

'Any foreign material left? Had she forgotten to take a tampon out?'

'No, but I still think I'm right.' Grace clicked a key. 'Yes… Her white count's sky high. So's her creatinine, which means she's got renal involvement. Could be septic shock from another cause but that won't change the initial management.'

'Plan?'

'More fluids, vasopressor support to try and get her BP up. And antibiotics, of course.'

'Flucloxacillin?'

'Yes. And I'll add in clindamycin. There's good evidence that it's effective in decreasing toxin production.' Grace looked past Charles to catch the attention of one of the nursing staff. 'Amy, could you see if there's a bed available in ICU, please? I've got a patient that's going to need intensive monitoring for a while.'

'On it, Dr Forbes.' The nurse reached for the phone.

Grace was gone, too, back to her patient. Charles gave up on the statistics. He would take them home and do his work later tonight, in those quiet hours after the boys were asleep. He was due to go and collect them soon, anyway.

Maybe he should give up on the idea of inviting Grace and Houston to join their party, too. He could give his boys everything they needed. He could take them out later today and let them choose the costumes they wanted themselves.

A sideways glance showed that Amy had finished her urgent arrangements for Grace's patient. She noticed his glance.

'Anything you need, Dr Davenport?'

He smiled at her. 'Not unless you happen to know of a good costume shop in this part of town?'

It seemed like every shop between Manhattan Mercy and home had decorated their windows for Halloween and it made Grace smile, despite her weariness after a couple of such busy days at work, to see the jack-o'-lanterns and ghosts and plastic spiders hanging on fluffy webs.

She'd missed this celebration in Australia.

As she turned towards the more residential area, there were groups of children already out, too, off to do their trick or treating in the late afternoon. So many excited little faces peeping out from beneath witches' hats or lions' ears, dancing along in pretty dresses with fairy wings on their backs or proudly being miniature superheroes.

What a shame that Charles hadn't taken her up on her subtle offer to share Halloween with him and his boys. She'd been thinking about him all day, and wondering just how difficult it had been for him when he had to be reliving every moment of this day three years ago when the twins had been born and he'd lost the love of his life.

Her heart was aching for Charles all over again, as she let herself into the apartment building, so it came as a surprise to hear a peal of laughter echoing down the tiled stairway with its wrought-iron bannisters.

The laughter of small people. And a deeper rumble of an adult male.

Grace paused in the foyer, looking upwards, and was rewarded by a small face she recognised instantly, peering down through the rails. His head was covered by a brown hood that had small round ears.

'*Gace*… Look at *us*…'

'I can't see you properly, Max.'

The face disappeared but she could still hear him.

'Daddy… *Daddy*…we have to visit Gace now…'

And there they were, coming down the stairs. Charles had hold of each twin's hand to keep them steady. In their other hands, the boys clutched a small, orange, plastic bucket shaped like a pumpkin. She could see plenty of candy in each bucket.

The brown hoods were part of a costume that covered them from head to toe.

'You're monkeys.' Grace grinned. 'But… where are your tails?'

The twins gave her a very patient look.

Charles gave her a shadow of a wink. 'Curious George doesn't have a tail,' he explained.

'Oh…'

'Trick or treat!' Cameron shouted. He bounced up and down on small padded feet. 'We want *candy*…'

'Please,' Charles admonished. 'Where are your manners, buddy?'

'Please!' It was Max who was first to comply.

'Grace might not have any candy. Maybe we could just say "hi" to Horse?'

'Actually, I *do* have some candy.' Grace smiled at Charles. 'I have a personal weakness for M&M'S. Would they be suitable?'

'A very small packet?' Charles was smiling back at her but looking slightly haunted. 'We already have enough candy to last till Christmas.'

'They're tiny boxes.' Grace pulled her keys

from her bag. 'Come on in. Horse will be so happy to see you.'

Charles had probably been in this apartment before, visiting Stefan and Jerome, but he hadn't come in since Grace had taken over and it felt like a huge step forward somehow. The huge, modern spaces had felt rather empty and totally not her style, although she was slowly getting used to them. With two small boys rolling around on the floor with Houston and Charles following her into the kitchen, it suddenly felt far more like a home.

'Let me open the French doors so that Houston can get out into the garden. It's been an hour or two since Kylie took him out for his last walk.' Grace headed for the pantry next, where she knew the big bag still had plenty of the small boxes of candy-covered chocolate she kept for an after-dinner treat.

She had a bottle of wine in the fridge, too. Would it be a step too far to offer one to Charles? She wanted to ask how the day had gone because she knew that she would be able to see past any cheerful accounts and know how hard it had really been. But she could see that anyway. Charles was looking tired and his smile didn't reach his eyes.

And she wasn't about to get the chance to

say anything, because his phone was ringing. He took the call, keeping an eye on the children, who were now racing around the garden with the dog, as he listened and then started firing questions.

'Who's there? How long ago did you activate Code Red?'

Grace caught her breath. 'Code Red' was a term used in Manhattan Mercy's ER to indicate that the level of patient numbers was exceeding the resources the department had to deal with them. Like a traffic light that was not functioning correctly, a traffic jam could ensue and, with patients, it meant that urgent treatment could be delayed and fatalities could result.

He listened a moment longer. 'I'll be there as soon as I can.'

'I can go back,' Grace offered as he ended the call. She could get there in less than ten minutes and she was still in her scrubs—she wouldn't even need to get changed.

But Charles shook his head. 'It's the administrative side that needs management. I'll have to go in.' He looked out at the garden. 'I can take the boys.'

This time, it was Grace who shook her head. 'Don't be daft. I'll look after them.'

Charles looked stunned by the offer. 'But...'

'But, nothing. I'll take them back up to your apartment. That way I can feed them. Or get them to bed if you end up being late. Is it okay if I take Houston up, too?'

'Of course...but...are you sure, Grace? They're going to get tired and cranky after the day they've had.'

Grace held his gaze. 'Go,' she said quietly. 'And don't worry about them. They'll be safe.'

For a heartbeat, she saw the shadows on his face lift as his smile very definitely reached his eyes.

'Thank you,' was all Charles said but it felt like she was the one who was being given something very special.

Trust?

CHAPTER FIVE

IF IT HADN'T been for her small entourage of two little boys and one large, fluffy dog, Grace might have felt like she was doing something wrong, stepping into Charles Davenport's private life like this.

How weird was it that just a few hours of one's lifetime, over a decade ago, could have had such an impact that it could make her feel like…like some kind of *stalker*?

It was her own fault. She had allowed herself to remember those hours. Enshrine them, almost, so that they had become a comfort zone that she had relied on, especially in the early days of coming to terms with what had felt like a broken and very lonely life. In those sleepless hours when things always seemed so much worse, she had imagined herself back in Charles's arms. Being held as though she was something precious.

Being made love to, as if she was the only woman in the world that Charles had wanted to be with.

She could have had a faceless fantasy to tap into but it had seemed perfectly safe to use Charles because she had never expected to see him again. And it had made it all seem so much more believable, because it *had* happened.

Once…

And, somewhere along the way, she had allowed herself to wonder about all the things she didn't know about him. What kind of house he lived in, for example. What his favourite food was. Whether he was married now and had a bunch of gorgeous kids.

She probably could have found out with a quick internet search but she never allowed those secret thoughts any head space in daylight hours. And, as soon as she'd started considering working at Manhattan Mercy, she had shut down even the familiar fantasy. It was no more than a very personal secret—a rather embarrassing one now.

But…entering his private domain like this was…

Satisfying?

Exciting?

Astonishing, certainly.

For some reason, she had expected it to be like the apartment she was living in on the ground floor of this wonderful, old building with its high ceilings and period features like original fireplaces and polished wooden floors. She had also expected the slightly overwhelming aura of wealth and style that Stefan and Jerome had created with their bespoke furniture and expertly displayed artworks.

The framework of the apartment with the floors and ceilings was no surprise but Grace's breath was taken away the moment she stepped through the door to face floor-to-ceiling windows that opened onto a terrace looking directly over Central Park. The polished floors didn't have huge Persian rugs like hers and the furniture looked like it had once been in a house out in the country somewhere. A big, old rambling farmhouse, maybe.

The couch was enormous and so well used that the leather looked crinkled and soft. There were picture books scattered over the rustic coffee table, along with crayons and paper and even the curling crust of an abandoned sandwich. There were toys all over the place, too—building bricks and brightly coloured cars, soft toy animals and half-done jigsaw puzzles.

It looked like...*home*...

The kind of home that was as much of a fantasy for Grace as being held—and loved—by someone totally genuine.

She had to swallow a huge lump in her throat.

And then she had to laugh, because Houston made a beeline for the coffee table and scoffed the old sandwich crust.

'I'm hungry,' Cameron announced, as he spotted the dog licking its lips.

'Me, too.' Max nodded.

Cameron upended his pumpkin bucket of candy onto the coffee table. Grace gave Houston a stern look that warned him to keep his nose out. Then she extracted the handfuls of candy from Cameron's fists.

'You can choose *one* thing,' she told him. 'But you can't eat it until after your dinner, okay?'

Cameron scowled at her. 'But I'm *hungry*.'

'I know.' Grace was putting the candy back into the bucket. 'Show me where the kitchen is and I'll make you some dinner. You'd better show me where the bathroom is, too.'

The twins led her into a spacious kitchen with a walk-in pantry.

'I'll show you,' Max offered.

He climbed onto a small step and wobbled precariously as he reached for something on a shelf. Grace caught him as he, and the packet he had triumphantly caught the edge of, fell off the step. For a moment, she stood there with the small, warm body in its fluffy monkey suit in her arms. She could smell the soft scent of something that was distinctly child-like. Baby shampoo, maybe?

Max giggled at the pleasure of being caught and, without thinking, Grace planted a kiss on his forehead.

'Down you go,' she said. 'And keep those monkey paws on the floor, where they're safe.'

She stooped to pick up the packet as she set him down.

'Mac and cheese? Is that what you guys want to eat?'

'Yes...*yes*...mac and cheese. For Horse, too...'

Houston waved his plume of a tail, clearly in agreement with the plan, but Grace was more dubious. She eyed the fruit bowl on the table in the kitchen and then the big fridge freezer. Could she tempt them to something healthier first—like an apple or a carrot? Were there some vegetables they might like in the freezer to go with the cheese and pasta? And packet pasta? *Really?* If she could find the ingredients, it wouldn't be hard to throw a fresh version in the oven. Cooking—and baking—were splinter skills she had enjoyed honing over the years.

The twins—and Horse—crowded around as she checked out what she might have to work with. There wasn't much in the way of fresh vegetables but the freezer looked well stocked.

'What's this?' The long cylindrical object was unfamiliar.

'Cookie dough,' Cameron told her. 'Maria makes us cookies.'

'Can you make cookies, Gace?' Max leaned forward so that he could turn his head to look up at her as she crouched. 'I *like* cookies.' Again, she had to catch him before he lost his balance and toppled into the freezer drawer.

'I don't see why not,' she decided. 'You can help. But only if you both eat an apple while I'm getting things ready. And we won't use the frozen sort. If there's some flour in the pantry and butter in the fridge, we'll make our own. From scratch.'

Over an hour later, Grace realised that the grand plan might have been ill-advised. This huge kitchen with its granite and stainless-steel work surfaces looked like a food bomb had been detonated and the sink was stacked with dirty pots and bowls. A fine snowstorm of flour had settled everywhere along with shreds of grated cheese and dribbles of chocolate icing. Houston had done his best to help and there wasn't a single crumb to be found on the floor, but he wasn't so keen on raw flour.

Whose idea had it been to make Halloween spider cookies?

The boys were sitting on the bench right now, on either side of the tray of cookies that had come out of the oven a short time ago. They had to be so tired by now, but they both had their hands clasped firmly in front of them, their eyes huge with excitement as they waited patiently for Grace to tell them it was safe to touch the hot cookies. It was so cute, she had to get her phone out and take a photo. Then she took a close-up of the cookies. The pale dough had made a perfect canvas for the iced chocolate spiders that had M&M eyes. She'd used a plastic bag to make a piping tool and had done her best to guide three-year-old hands to position spider legs but the results were haphazard. One spider appeared to be holding its eyes on the ends of a very fat leg.

Should she send one of the photos to Charles?

A closer glance at the image of his sons

made her decide not to. Still in their monkey suits, the boys now had chocolate smears on their faces and the curls of Max's hair that had escaped his hood had something that looked like cheese sauce in it. Her own hair had somehow escaped its fastenings recently and she was fairly sure that she would find a surprise or two when she tried to brush it later.

Hopefully, she would have time to clean up before their father got home but the children and the kitchen would have to take priority. Not wanting to look a wreck in front of Charles was no excuse to worry about her own appearance. She was still in her work scrubs, for heaven's sake—what did it matter?

She prodded one of the cookies.

'Still too hot, guys,' she said. 'But our mac and cheese has cooled down. You can have some of that and then the cookies will be ready for dessert.'

She lifted one twin and then the other off the bench. 'Do you want to take your monkey suits off now?'

'No. We want to be George.'

'And *watch* George,' Max added, nodding his agreement.

'Okay. Do you eat your dinner at the table?'

'Our table,' Cameron told her. 'With TV.'

'Hmm. Let's wash those monkey paws.'

Grace wasn't sure that eating in front of the television was really the norm but, hey… they were all tired now and it was a birthday, after all. She served bowls of the homemade pasta bake on the top of a small, bright yellow table that Cameron and Max dragged to be right in front of the widescreen television. The chairs were different primary shades and had the boys' names painted on the back. Fortunately, it was easy to see how to use the DVD player and an episode of *Curious George* was already loaded.

The smell of the mac and cheese made Grace realise how hungry she was herself. She knew she should tackle the mess in the kitchen but it wouldn't hurt to curl up on the couch with a bowl of food for a few minutes, would it?

The yellow table, and the bowls, were suspiciously clean when Grace came in later with the platter of cookies and Houston had an innocent air that looked well practised. She had to press her lips together not to laugh out loud. She needed some practice of her own, perhaps, in good parenting?

The thought caught her unawares. She'd been enjoying this time so much it hadn't occurred to her to realise that she was living a fantasy. But that was good, wasn't it? That day at the park, she had wanted to able to embrace a special moment for what it was and not ruin it by remembering old pain. She had done that with bells on with this unexpected babysitting job.

The laughter had evaporated, though. And her smile felt distinctly wobbly. It was just as well that Cameron turned his head to notice what she was carrying.

'Cookies...'

Max's chair fell over backwards in his haste to get up and Houston barked his approval of the new game as they all rushed at Grace. She sat on the couch with a bump and held the platter too high to be reached by all those small fingers.

'One each,' she commanded. 'And none for Horse, okay?'

They ended up having two each but they weren't overly big cookies. And the crumbs didn't really matter because a leather couch would be easy enough to clean. Not that Grace wanted to move just yet. She had two small boys nestled on either side of her and they were all mesmerised by what Curious George was up to on the screen.

'He's a very naughty monkey, isn't he? Look at all that paint he's spilling everywhere!'

The boys thought it was hilarious but she could feel their warm bodies getting heavier and heavier against her own. Houston was sound asleep with his head pillowed on her feet and Grace could feel her own eyes drooping. Full of comfort food and suddenly exhausted by throwing herself so enthusiastically into what would undoubtedly become an emotionally charged memory, it was impossible not to let herself slip into a moment of putting off the inevitable return to reality.

She wouldn't let herself fall asleep, of course. She would just close her eyes and sink into this group cuddle for a minute or two longer...

It was the last thing Charles had expected to see when he let himself quietly into his apartment late that evening.

He knew his boys would have crashed hours ago and he had assumed they would be tucked up in their shared bedroom, in the racing car beds that had been last year's extravagant gift from their grandparents.

They were, indeed, fast asleep when he arrived home after his hectic troubleshooting in a stretched emergency department, but they weren't in their own beds. Or even in their pyjamas. Still encased in their little monkey suits, Cameron and Max were curled up like puppies on either side of Grace, who was also apparently sound asleep on the couch. Houston had woken at the scratch of the key in the lock, of course, but he wasn't about to abandon the humans he was protecting. He didn't budge from where he was lying across Grace's feet but he seemed to be smiling up at Charles and his tail was twitching in a muted wag.

It might have been a totally unexpected sight, but it was also the cutest thing Charles had ever seen. He gazed at the angelic, sleeping faces of his sons and could feel his heart expanding with love so much it felt like it was in danger of bursting. They were both tucked under a protective arm. Grace had managed to stay sitting upright in her sleep but her head was tilted to one side. He had never seen her face in slumber and she looked far younger than the thirty-six years he knew she shared with him. Far more vulnerable than she ever looked when she was awake.

Maybe it was because she was a single unit with his boys at the moment that she was automatically included in this soft wash of feeling so protective.

So…blessed?

But then Charles stepped closer. What was that in Grace's hair? And smeared on her cheek?

Chocolate?

A closer glance at the twins revealed unexplained substances in odd places as well. Charles could feel his face crease into a deep frown. What on earth had been going on here? Walking quietly, he went through the sitting room towards the kitchen and it wasn't long before he stopped in his tracks, utterly stunned.

He'd never seen a mess like this.

Ever…

His feet were leaving prints in the layer of flour on the floor. The sink was overflowing with dirty dishes. There was a deep dish half-full of what looked like mac and cheese and a wire rack that was covered with cookies. Cookies that were decorated with…good grief… what were those strange blobs and squiggles with chocolate candies poked amongst them?

Ah…there was one with a recognisable shape.

A spider…

And then it hit Charles. Grace had been

making Halloween cookies with the boys and clearly she had let them do most of the decorating themselves.

Suddenly, the appalling mess in the kitchen ceased to matter because Charles had glimpsed a much bigger picture. One that caught his heart in a very different way to seeing his boys sleeping so contentedly.

This was a kind of scene that he had never envisaged in the lives of his precious little family. Because it was a dimension that only a woman would think of including?

A *mother*?

Somehow, it wrapped itself into the whole idea of a home. Of a kitchen being the heart of the house. Of putting up with unnecessary mess because that was how children learned important things. Not just about how to make cookies but about…about *home*.

About being safe. And loved.

For a moment, the feeling was overwhelming enough to bring a lump to his throat and a prickle to the back of his eyes that brought all sorts of other sensations in their wake.

Feelings of loss.

And longing…

He had to cradle his forehead between his

thumb and finger and rub hard at his temples to stop himself falling into a complete wreck.

It was too much. On top of such an emotionally charged day riding that roller-coaster between remembered grief and the very real celebration of his boys' lives, topped off with an exhausting few hours of high-powered management of a potentially dangerous situation, it was no wonder this was overwhelming.

It was too much.

But it was also kind of perfect.

It was the gentle extraction of a small body from beneath her arm that woke Grace.

For a moment, she blinked sleepily up at Charles, thinking that she was dreaming.

That *smile*...

She had never seen anything quite so tender.

He was smiling at her as if he loved her as much as she knew he loved his children.

Yep. Definitely a dream.

But then Max gave a tiny whimper in his sleep as he was lifted. And the warm weight on her feet shifted as Houston got up and then it all came rushing back to Grace.

'Oh, my God...' she whispered. 'I fell asleep. Oh, Charles, I'm *so* sorry...'

'Don't be.'

'But the *mess*. I was going to clean it all up before you got home.'

'Shh…' Charles was turning away, a still sleeping Max cradled in his arms. 'I'll put Max down and then come back for Cameron. Don't move, or you might wake him up.'

That gave Grace all the time she needed to remember exactly what state she'd left this beautiful apartment in. It was bad enough in here, with the television still going, scattered toys and dinner dishes where they'd been left, but the kitchen…

Oh, help… She'd been given total responsibility and she had created a complete disaster.

But Charles didn't seem to mind. He lifted Cameron with a gentleness that took her breath away. Maybe because his hands brushed her own body as he slid them into place and she could feel just how much care he was taking not to wake his son. His gaze caught hers as she lifted her arm to make his task easier and, amazingly, he was still smiling.

As if he didn't actually care about the mess.

Grace cared. She got to her feet and any residual fuzziness from being woken from a deep sleep evaporated instantly as she went back to the kitchen.

It was even worse than she'd remembered.

Should she start with that pile of unwashed dishes or find a broom and start sweeping the floor?

Reaching out, she touched a puddle of chocolate icing on the granite surface of the work bench. It had hardened enough that it would need a lot more than a cloth to wipe it clean. Where were the cleaning supplies kept? Grace pushed her hair back from her face as she looked around and, to her horror, she found a hard lump that had glued a large clump of hair together. Hard enough to suggest it was more chocolate icing.

She was still standing there, mortified, when Charles came to find her.

For a long moment, she couldn't think of anything to say that could encompass how embarrassed she was. Finally, she had to risk making eye contact. He had to be furious, surely, even if he'd been doing a superb job of hiding it so far.

He caught her gaze and held it firmly. Grace couldn't look away.

Yes…there was something stern enough there to let her know he knew exactly how major the clean-up job would be. That he knew how carried away she'd been in her attempt to keep the twins entertained. That she'd surprised him, to say the very least.

But there was something else there as well.

A...twinkle...

Of amusement, laced with something else.

Appreciation maybe.

No...it was deeper than that. Something she couldn't identify.

'What?' she heard herself whisper. 'What are you thinking? That you'll never leave me in charge of your kids again?'

One corner of his mouth lifted into a smile that could only be described as poignant.

'I'm thinking,' he said quietly. 'That I've spent the last three years trying to be both a father and a mother to my kids and keep their lives as predictable and safe as I can and then someone comes in and, in the space of a few hours, wrecks my house and shows me exactly what I didn't realise was missing.'

Grace's brain had fixed on the comment about wrecking his house.

'I'm sorry,' she murmured.

Charles's gaze shifted a fraction. Oh, help... was he staring at the lump of chocolate icing in her hair?

'I've never even thought of making cookies with the boys,' he said. 'I wouldn't know where to start. I know Maria makes them sometimes, but all that's involved there is slicing up a frozen roll and sticking them in the oven. I'm surprised you even found a bag of flour in the pantry. Not only that, you let them draw spiders on the top.'

'Oh…' Grace could feel her lips curve with pleasure. 'You could tell what they were, then?'

'Only after I spotted one that you probably did. Some of them seem to have eyes on their legs.'

'Helps to see round corners,' Grace suggested. Her smile widened.

Charles was smiling back at her and that twinkle in his eyes had changed into something else.

Something that was giving her a very distinctive shaft of sensation deep in her belly.

Attraction, that's what it was.

A very physical and very definite attraction.

Maybe Charles was feeling it, too. Maybe that was why he lifted his hand to touch her hair.

'Chocolate,' he told her.

'I know…' Grace made a face. 'You might find you need to wash the boys' hair in the morning as well.'

'It's not a problem.' Charles was touching

her cheek now, his finger feather-light. 'You've got some here, too.'

Grace couldn't say anything. She was shocked by the touch and the electricity of the current it was producing that flashed through her body like a lightning bolt to join the pool of sensation lower down.

The smile on Charles's face was fading fast. For another one of those endless moments, they stared at each other again.

Fragments of unformed thoughts bombarded Grace. Memories of another time when they'd looked at each other just like this. Before Charles had kissed her for the very first time. Snatches of the conversation they'd just had. What had he meant when he'd said that she'd shown him what he hadn't realised was missing in his life?

Surely he didn't mean *her*?

Part of her really wanted that to have been the meaning.

The part that held his gaze, willing him to make the first move…

He was still touching her cheek but his finger moved past any smear of chocolate, tracing the edge of her nose and then out to the corner of her mouth and along her bottom lip.

And then he shut his eyes as he bent his

head, taking his finger away just before his lips took its place.

Another shock wave of unbearably exquisite pleasure shot through Grace's body and she had to close her own eyes as she fell into it.

Dear Lord…she had relived a kiss from this man so many times in her imagination but somehow the reality had been muted over the years.

Nobody else had ever kissed her like this. Ever…

It was impossible not to respond. To welcome the deepening of that kiss. To press herself closer to the remembered planes of that hard, lean body. It wasn't until his hand shifted from her back to slide under her ribs and up onto her breast that Grace was suddenly blindsided by reality.

By what Charles was about to touch.

She could feel the adrenaline flood her body now, her muscles tensing instantly in a classic fight-or-flight reflex, in the same moment that she jerked herself back.

Charles dropped his hand instantly. Stepped back from the kiss just as swiftly.

And this time there was a note of bewilderment in his eyes. Of horror, even…

They both looked away.

'Um...' Grace struggled to find her voice. And a reason to escape. 'I...I really need to take Houston downstairs. He must be a bit desperate to get out by now.'

'Of course.' Was it her imagination or did Charles seem grateful for an excuse to ignore what had just happened? 'He needs his garden.'

'I can't leave you with this mess, though.'

'My cleaner's due in the morning. It really isn't a problem.'

No. Grace swallowed hard. They had another problem now, though, didn't they?

But she could feel the distance between them accelerating. She wasn't the only one who needed to escape, was she?

They hadn't just crossed a barrier here. They had smashed through it with no consideration of any repercussions.

And maybe they were just as big for Charles as they were for herself.

But Grace couldn't afford to feel any empathy right now. The need to protect herself was too overwhelming.

With no more than a nod to acknowledge her being excused from cleaning up the mess she had created, Grace took her leave and fled downstairs with Houston.

She had no mental space to feel guilty about escaping.

Besides, Charles had created a bit of a mess himself, hadn't he? By kissing her like that.

That was more than enough to deal with for the moment.

CHAPTER SIX

'OH, MY...' VANESSA DAVENPORT looked slightly appalled as she peered more closely at what was being held up for her admiration. 'What *are* they?'

'Cookies, Grandma.' Cameron was using that patient tone that told adults they were being deliberately obtuse. 'We *made* them.'

'And Gace,' Max added.

'Gace?' Vanessa was looking bewildered now but Charles didn't offer an explanation.

He was kicking himself inwardly. He should have known exactly what his mother's reaction would be to the less than perfect cookies, but he couldn't forgive the slap to his boys' pride that had prompted them to insist on bringing their creations to the family afternoon tea.

It was the complete opposite end to the spectrum that Grace was also on. She'd been just as proud of the boys at the results of their efforts. This morning, she'd sent him the photo she'd taken of them sitting on the bench, their hands clasped and eyes shining with the tray of cookies between them. It even had Horse's nose photobombing the bottom of the image and Charles had been so taken with it, he'd thought of using it for his Christmas cards this year.

Maybe not, if his mother was going to look like this.

'Let's give them to Alice.' Vanessa was an expert in ignoring anything that she didn't approve of. 'She can put them in the kitchen.'

Alice was hovering in the background, ready to help with hanging coats up in the cloakroom, but she moved swiftly when there was another knock on the massive front door of the Davenport mansion. His father, Hugo, was coming into the foyer at the same time and the twins' faces brightened.

'Look, Grandpa...look what we made.'

'Wow...cookies...they look delicious.'

'Did I hear someone mention cookies?'

Charles turned towards the door. 'Miranda. Hey... I'm glad you could make it.'

His half-sister had two brightly wrapped parcels under her arm and the twins' eyes got very round.

'Presents, Daddy. For us?'

But Charles had been distracted by someone who had followed Miranda into the house. He hadn't seen his youngest brother, Zachary, for such a long time.

'Zac... What are you doing here?'

'I heard there was a birthday celebration happening.'

'But I thought you were in Annapolis.'

'I was. I am. I'm just in town for the day— you should know why...'

Charles had to shake his head but there was no time to ask. The shriek of excitement behind him had to mean that Miranda had handed over the parcels and, turning his head, he could see his mother already moving towards the main reception lounge.

'For goodness' sake,' she said. 'Let's go somewhere a little more civilised than the doorstep, shall we?'

Charles saw the glance that flashed between Zac and Miranda. Would there ever come a day when Vanessa actually welcomed Miranda into this house, instead of barely tolerating her?

His father was now holding the platter of cookies.

'Shall I take those to the kitchen, sir?' Alice asked.

'No…no…they have to go on the table with all the other treats.'

Charles felt a wash of relief. Families were always complicated and this one a lot more than most but there was still a thread of something good to be found. Something worth celebrating.

He scooped up Cameron, who was already ripping the paper off his gift. 'Hang on, buddy. Let's do that in the big room.'

Zac had parcels in his hands, too. And when the door swung open behind him to reveal Elijah with a single, impressively large box in his arms, Charles could only hope that this gathering wasn't going to be too overwhelming for small boys. He thought wistfully of the relatively calm oasis of their own apartment and, unbidden, an image of the ultimately peaceful scene he'd come home to last night filled his mind.

The one of Grace, asleep on the couch, cuddled up with the boys and with a dog asleep on her feet.

So peaceful. So…perfect…?

'I can't stay,' Elijah said, as they all started moving to the lounge. 'I got someone to cover me for an hour at work. I'll be getting a taxi back in half an hour.'

'Oh…' Miranda was beside him. 'Could I share? My shift starts at five but it takes so long on the Tube I'd have to leave about then, anyway.'

'Flying visit,' Zac murmured. 'It's always the way with us Davenports, isn't it? Do your duty but preferably with an excuse to escape before things get awkward?'

'Mmm.' The sound was noncommittal but Charles put Cameron down with an inward sigh. This vast room, with a feature fireplace and enough seating for forty people, had obviously been professionally decorated. Huge, helium balloons were tethered everywhere and there were streamers looping between the chandeliers and a banner covering the wall behind the mahogany dining table that had been shifted in here from the adjoining dining room. A table that was laden with perfectly decorated cakes and cookies and any number of other delicious treats that had been provided by professional caterers.

Cameron, with his half-unwrapped parcel in his arms, ran towards the pile of other gifts near the table, Max hot on his heels. A maid he didn't recognise came towards the adults with a silver tray laden with flutes of champagne.

'Orange juice for me, thanks,' Elijah said. Miranda just shook her head politely and went after the twins to help them with the unwrapping.

'So what's with your flying visit?' he asked Zac. 'And why should I know about it?'

'Because I'm here for an interview. I've applied for a job at Manhattan Mercy that starts next month.'

'Really? Wow…' Charles took a sip of his champagne. 'That's great, man. And there I was thinking you were going to be a navy medic for the rest of your life.'

Zac shrugged. 'Maybe I'm thinking that life's short, you know? If I don't get around to building some bridges soon, it's never going to happen.'

Charles could only nod. He knew better than anyone how short life could be, didn't he? About the kind of jagged hole that could be left when someone you loved got ripped from it.

But that hole had been covered last night, hadn't it? Just for a moment or two, he had stepped far enough away from it for it to have become invisible. And it had been that perfect family scene that had led him away. His

two boys, under the sheltering arms of someone who had looked, for all the world, like
their mother. With a loyal family pet at their
feet, even.

But now Zac had shown him the signpost
that led straight back to the gaping hole in his
life.

And Elijah was shaking his head. 'I hope
you're not harbouring any hope of this lot playing happy families any time soon.'

They all turned their gazes on their parents. Hugo and Miranda were both down on
the floor with the twins. Miranda's gifts of a
new toy car for Cameron and a tractor for Max
had been opened and set aside and now the
first of the many parcels from the grandparents were being opened. It looked like it was a
very large train set, judging by the lengths of
wooden rails that were appearing. The level of
excitement was increasing and Charles needed
to go and share it. Maybe that way, the twins
wouldn't notice the way their grandmother was
perched on a sofa at some distance, merely
watching the spectacle.

'Anyone else coming?' Zac asked. 'Where's
Penny?'

'Still on holiday. Skiing, I think. Or was it
sky-diving?'

'Sounds like her. And Jude? I'd love to catch up with him.'

'Are you kidding?' Elijah's eyebrows rose. 'Being a cousin is a perfect "get out of jail" card for most of our family get-togethers.'

Charles moved away from his brothers. It was always like this. Yes, there were moments of joy to be found in his family but the undercurrents were strong enough to mean that there was always tension. And most of that tension came from Vanessa and Elijah.

You had to make allowances, of course. It was his mother who'd been hardest hit by the scandal of learning that her husband had been having an affair that had resulted in a child—Miranda. That knowledge would have been hard enough, but to find out because Miranda's mother had died and her father had insisted on acknowledging her and bringing her into the family home had been unbearable for Vanessa.

Unbearable for everyone. The difference in age between himself and his twin might have been insignificant but Charles had always known that he was the oldest child. The first-born. And that came with a responsibility that he took very seriously. That turbulent period of the scandal had been his first real test and he'd done everything he could to comfort his siblings—especially Elijah, who'd been so angry and bitter. To protect the frightened teenager who had suddenly become one of their number as well. And to support his devastated mother, who was being forced to start an unexpected chapter in her life.

Like the authors of many of the gossip columns, he'd expected his mother would walk away from her marriage but Vanessa had chosen not to take that option. She'd claimed that she didn't want to bring more shame on the Davenport family but they all knew that what scared her more would have been walking away from her own exalted position in New York society and the fundraising efforts that had become her passion.

To outward appearances, the shocking changes had been tolerated with extraordinary grace. Behind closed doors, however, it had been a rather different story. There were no-go areas that Vanessa had constructed for her own protection and nobody, including her husband, would dream of intruding on them uninvited.

Charles had always wondered if he could have done more, especially for Elijah, who had ended up so bitter about marriage and what he sarcastically referred to as 'happy families'.

If he could have done a better job as the first-born, maybe he could have protected his family more successfully, perhaps by somehow diverting the destructive force of the scandal breaking. It hadn't been his fault, of course, any more than Nina's death had been. Why didn't that lessen the burden that a sense of responsibility created?

But surely enough time had passed to let them all move on?

Charles felt tired of it all suddenly. The effort it had taken to try and keep his shattered family together would have been all-consuming at any time. To have had it happen in the run-up to his final exams had been unbelievably difficult. Life-changing.

If it hadn't happened, right after that night he'd shared with Grace, how different might his life have been?

Would he have shut her out so completely? Pretended that night had never happened because that was a factor he had absolutely no head space to even consider?

To his shame, Charles had been so successful in shutting it out in that overwhelmingly stressful period, he had never thought of how it might have hurt Grace.

Was *that* why she'd pretty much flinched

during that kiss last night? Why she'd practically run away from him as hard and fast as she could politely manage?

Receiving that photo this morning had felt kind of like Grace was sending an olive branch. An apology for running, perhaps. Or at least an indication that they could still be friends?

The effect was a swirl of confusion. He had glimpsed something huge that was missing from his life, along with the impression that Grace was possibly the only person who could fill that gap. The very edges of that notion should be stirring his usual reaction of disloyalty to Nina that thoughts of including any other woman in his life usually engendered.

But it wasn't happening…

Because there was a part of his brain that was standing back and providing a rather different perspective? Would Nina have wanted her babies to grow up without a mom?

Would *he* have wanted them to grow up without a dad, if he'd been the one to die too soon?

Of course not.

He had experienced the first real surge of physical desire in three long years, too. That should be sparking the guilt but it didn't seem to be. Not in the way he'd become so accustomed to, anyway.

He wouldn't have inflicted a life of celibacy on Nina, either.

Maybe the guilt was muted by something more than a different perspective. Because, after the way she had reacted last night, it seemed that going any further down that path was very unlikely?

The more he thought about it, the more his curiosity about Grace was intensifying.

She had felt the same level of need, he knew she had. She had responded to that kiss in a way that had inflamed that desire to a mind-blowing height.

And then she'd flinched as though he had caused her physical pain.

Why?

It wasn't really any of his business but curiosity was becoming a need to know.

Because, as unlikely as it was, could the small part he had played in Grace's life in the past somehow have contributed to whatever it was?

A ridiculous notion but, if nothing else, it seemed like a legitimate reason to try and find out the truth. Not that it was going to be easy, mind you. Some people were very good at building walls to keep their pain private. Like his mother. Thanks to that enormous effort he'd made to try and keep his family together during the worst time of that scandal breaking, however, he had learned more than anyone about exactly what was behind Vanessa Davenport's walls. Because he'd respected that pain and had had a base of complete trust to work from.

He could hardly expect Grace to trust him that much. Not when he looked back over the years and could see the way he'd treated her from her point of view.

But there was something there.

And, oddly, it did *feel* a bit like trust.

Stepping over train tracks that his father was slotting together, smiling at the delight on his sons' faces as they unwrapped a bright blue steam engine with a happy face on the front, Charles moved towards the couch and bent to kiss Vanessa's cheek.

'Awesome present, Mom,' he said with a smile. 'Clever of you to know how much the boys love Thomas the Tank Engine.'

That kiss had changed everything.

Only a few, short weeks ago Grace had been so nervous about meeting Charles Davenport again that she had almost decided against applying for the job at Manhattan Mercy.

What had she been so afraid of? That old feelings might resurface and she'd have to suffer the humiliation of being dismissed so completely again?

To find that the opposite had happened was even scarier. That old connection was still there and could clearly be tapped into but... Grace didn't want that.

Well...she *did*...but she wasn't ready.

She might never be ready.

Charles must think she was crazy. He must have sensed the connection at the same moment she had, when they'd shared their amusement about the spiders that had eyes on their legs, otherwise he wouldn't have touched her like that.

And he must have seen that fierce shaft of desire because she had felt it throughout her entire body so why wouldn't it have shown in her eyes?

Just for those few, deliciously long moments she had been unaware of anything but that desire when he'd kissed her. That spiralling need for more.

And then his hand had—almost—touched

her breast and she'd reacted as if he'd pulled a knife on her or something.

It had been purely instinctive and Grace knew how over the top it must have seemed. She was embarrassed.

A bit ashamed of herself, to be honest, but there it was. A trigger that had been too deeply set to be disabled.

The net effect was to make her feel even more nervous about her next meeting with Charles than she had been about the first one and he hadn't been at work the next day so her anxiety kept growing.

She had sent out mixed messages and he had every right to be annoyed with her. How awkward would it be to work together from now on? Did she really want to live with a resurrection of all the reasons why she'd taken herself off to work in the remotest places she could find?

No. What she wanted was to wind back the clock just a little. To the time before that kiss, when it had felt like an important friendship was being cemented. When she had discovered a totally unexpected dimension in her life by embracing a sense of family in her time with Charles and his sons and Houston.

So she had sent through that photo she had

taken of Max and Cameron waiting for the cookies to cool. Along with another apology for the mess they had all created. Maybe she wanted to test the waters and see just how annoyed he might be.

He had texted back to thank her, and say that it was one of the best photos of the boys he'd ever seen. He also said that they were going to a family birthday celebration that afternoon and surprised her by saying he didn't think it would be nearly as much fun as baking Halloween cookies.

A friendly message—as if nothing had changed.

The relief was welcome.

But confusing.

Unless Charles was just as keen as she was to turn the clock back?

Of course he was, she decided by the end of that day, as she took Houston for a long, solitary walk in the park. He had as big a reason as she did not to want to get that close to someone. He had lost the absolute love of his life under horrifically traumatic circumstances. Part of him had to want to keep on living— as she did—and not to be deprived of the best things that life had to offer.

But maybe he wasn't ready yet, either.

Maybe he never would be.

And that was okay—because maybe they could still be friends and that was something that could be treasured.

Evidence that Charles wanted to push the 'reset' button on their friendship came at increasingly frequent intervals over the next week or two. Now that his nanny, Maria, had recovered from her back injury enough to work during week days, he was in the emergency room every day that Grace was working.

He gave her a printed copy of the photograph, during a quiet moment when they both happened to be near the unit desk on one occasion.

'Did you see that Horse photobombed it?'

Grace laughed. 'No…I thought I'd had my thumb on the lens or something. I was going to edit it out.'

She wouldn't now. She would tuck this small picture into her wallet and she knew that sometimes she would take it out and look at it. A part of her would melt with love every time. And part of her would splinter into little pieces and cry?

She avoided looking directly at Charles as she slipped the image carefully into her pocket.

'Did your cleaning lady resign the next day?'

'No. She wants the recipe for your home-made mac and cheese.'

It was unfortunate that Grace glanced at Charles as he stopped speaking to lick his lips. That punch of sensation in her belly was a warning that friendship with this man would never be simple. Or easy. That it could become even worse, in fact, because there might come a time when she was ready to take that enormous step into a new life only to find that Charles would never feel the same way.

'I'd like it, too.' He didn't seem to have noticed that she was edging away. 'I had some later that night and it was the most delicious thing ever. It had *bacon* in it.'

'Mmm… It's not hard.'

'Maybe you could show me. Sometime…'

The suggestion was casual but Grace had to push an image from her mind of standing beside Charles as she taught him how to make a cheese sauce. Of being close enough to touch him whilst wrapped in the warmth and smells of a kitchen—the heart of a home. She could even feel a beat of the fear that being so close would bring and she had to swallow hard.

'I'll write down how to do it for you.'

Charles smiled and nodded but seemed

distracted now. He was staring at the patient details board. 'What's going on with that patient in Curtain Six? She's been here for a long time.'

'We're waiting for a paediatric psyche consult. This is her third admission in a week. Looks like a self-inflicted injury and I think there's something going on at home that she's trying to escape from.'

'Oh...' His breath was a sigh. 'Who brought her in?'

'Her stepfather. And he's very reluctant to leave her alone with staff.'

'Need any help?'

'I think we're getting there. I've told him that we need to run more tests. Might even have to keep her in overnight for observation. I know we've blocked up a bed for too long, but...'

'Don't worry about it.' The glance Grace received was direct. Warm. 'Do whatever you need to do. I trust you. Just let me know if you need backup.'

Feeling trusted was a powerful thing.

Knowing that you had the kind of backup that could also be trusted was even better and Grace was particularly grateful for that a couple of mornings later with the first case that arrived on her shift.

A thirteen-month-old boy, who had somehow managed to crawl out of the house at some point during the night and had been found, virtually frozen solid, in the back yard.

'VF arrest,' the paramedics had radioed in. 'CPR under way. We can't intubate—his mouth's frozen. We've just got an OPA in.'

Grace had the team ready in their resuscitation area.

'We need warmed blankets and heat packs. Warmed IV fluids. We'll be looking at thoracic lavage or even ECMO. Have we heard back from the cardiac surgical team yet?'

'Someone's on their way.'

'ECMO?' she heard a nurse whisper. 'What's that?'

'Extra corporeal membrane oxygenation,' she told them. 'It's a form of cardiopulmonary bypass and we can warm the blood at the same time. Because, like we've all been taught, you're not—'

'—dead until you're warm and dead.'

It was Charles who finished her sentence for her, as he appeared beside her, pushing his arms through the sleeves of a gown. He didn't smile at her, but there was a crinkle at the corners of his eyes that gave her a boost of confidence.

'Thought you might like a hand,' he murmured. 'We've done this before, remember?'

Grace tilted her head in a single nod of acknowledgement. She was focused on the gurney being wheeled rapidly towards them through the doors. Of course she remembered. It had been the only time she and Charles had worked so closely together during those long years of training. They had been left to deal with a case of severe hypothermia in an overstretched emergency department when they had been no more than senior medical students. Their patient had been an older homeless woman that nobody had seemed to want to bother with.

They had looked at each other and quietly chanted their new mantra in unison.

'You're not dead until you're warm and dead.'

And they'd stayed with her, taking turns to change heat packs and blankets while keeping up continuous CPR for more than ninety minutes. Until her body temperature was high enough for defibrillation to be an effective option.

Nobody ever forgot the first time they defibrillated somebody.

Especially when it was successful.

But this was very different. This wasn't an elderly woman who might not have even been missed if she had succumbed to her hypothermia. This was a precious child who had distraught members of his family watching their every move. A tiny body that looked, and felt, as if it was made of chilled wax as he was gently transferred to the heated mattress, where his soaked, frozen nappy was removed and heat packs were nestled under his arms and in his groin.

'Pupils?'

'Fixed and dilated.'

Grace caught Charles's gaze as she answered his query and it was no surprise that she couldn't see any hint of a suggestion that it might be too late to help this child. It was more an acknowledgement that the battle had just begun. That they'd done this before and they could do it again. And they might be surrounded by other staff members but it almost felt like it was just them again. A tight team, bonded by an enormous challenge and the determination to succeed.

Finding a vein to start infusing warmed

IV fluids presented a challenge they didn't have time for so Grace used an intraosseous needle to place a catheter inside the tibia where the bone marrow provided a reliable connection to the central circulation. It was Charles who took over the chest compressions from the paramedics and initiated the start of warmed oxygen for ventilation and then it was Elijah who stepped in to continue while Charles and Grace worked together to intubate and hook the baby up to the ventilator.

The cardiac surgical team arrived soon after that, along with the equipment that could be used for more aggressive internal warming, by direct cannulation of major veins and arteries to both warm the blood and take over the work of the heart and lungs or the procedure of infusing the chest cavity with warmed fluids and then draining it off again. If ECMO or bypass was going to be used, the decision had to be made whether to do it here in the department or move their small patient to Theatre.

'How long has CPR been going?'

'Seventy-five minutes.'

'Body temperature?'

'Twenty-two degrees Celsius. Up from twenty-one on arrival. It was under twenty on scene.'

'Rhythm?'

'Still ventricular fibrillation.'

'Has he been shocked?'

'Once. On scene.' Again, it was Charles's gaze that Grace sought. 'We were waiting to get his temperature up a bit more before we tried again but maybe…'

'It's worth a try,' one of the cardiac team said. 'Before we start cannulation.'

But it was the nod from Charles that Grace really wanted to see before she pushed the charge button on the defibrillator.

'Stand clear,' she warned as crescendo of sound switched to a loud beeping. 'Shocking now.'

It was very unlikely that one shock would convert the fatal rhythm into one that was capable of pumping blood but, to everyone's astonishment, that was exactly what it did. Charles had his fingers resting gently near a tiny elbow.

'I've got a pulse.'

'Might not last,' the surgeon warned. 'He's still cold enough for it to deteriorate back into VF at any time, especially if he's moved.'

Grace nodded. 'We won't move him. Let's keep on with what we're doing with active external rewarming and ventilation. We'll add in some inotropes as well.'

'It could take hours.' The surgeon looked at his watch. 'I can't stay, I'm afraid. I've got a theatre list I'm already late for but page me if you run into trouble.'

Charles nodded but the glance he gave Grace echoed what she was thinking herself. They had won the first round of this battle and, together, they would win the next.

There wasn't much that they could do, other than keep up an intensive monitoring that meant not stepping away from this bedside. Heat packs were refreshed and body temperature crept up, half a degree at a time. There were blood tests to run and drugs to be cautiously administered. They could let the parents come in for a short time to see what was happening and to reassure them that everything possible was being done but they couldn't be allowed to touch their son yet. The situation was still fragile and only time would give them the answers they all needed.

His name, they learned, was Toby.

It wasn't necessary to have two senior doctors present the whole time but neither Charles nor Grace gave any hint of wanting to be anywhere else and, fortunately, there were enough staff to cover everything else that was happening in the department.

More than once, they were the only people in the room with Toby. Their conversation was quiet and professional, focused solely on the challenge they were dealing with and, at first, any eye contact was that of colleagues. Encouraging. Appreciative. Hopeful…

It was an odd bubble to be in, at the centre of a busy department but isolated at the same time. And when it was just the two of them, when a nurse left to deliver blood samples or collect new heat packs, there was an atmosphere that Grace could only describe as… peaceful?

No. That wasn't the right word. It felt as though she was a piece of a puzzle that was complete enough to see what the whole picture was going to be. There were only a few pieces still to fit into the puzzle and they were lying close by, waiting to be picked up. It was a feeling of trust that went a step beyond hope. It was simply a matter of time.

So perhaps that was why those moments of eye contact changed as one hour morphed into the next. Why it was so hard to look away, because that was when she could feel it the most—that feeling that the puzzle was going to be completed and that it was a picture she had been waiting her whole life to see.

It felt like…happiness.

Nearly three hours later, Toby was declared stable enough to move to the paediatric intensive care unit. He was still unconscious but his heart and other organs were functioning normally again. Whether he had suffered any brain damage would not be able to be assessed until he woke up.

If he woke up?

Was that why Grace was left with the feeling that she hadn't quite been able to reach those last puzzle pieces? Why the picture she wanted to see so badly was still a little blurred?

No. The way Charles was looking at her as Toby's bed disappeared through the internal doors of the ER assured Grace that she had done the best job she could and, for now, the outcome was the best it could possibly be. That he was proud of her. Proud of his department.

And then he turned to start catching up with the multitude of tasks that had accumulated and needed his attention. Grace watched him walking away from her and that was when instinct kicked in.

That puzzle wasn't really about a patient at all, was it?

It was about herself.

And Charles.

CHAPTER SEVEN

'BIT COLD FOR the park today, isn't it, Doc?
They're sayin' it could snow.'

'I know, but the boys are desperate for a
bike ride. We haven't been able to get outside
to play for days.'

Jack brightened at the prospect of leaving
the tiny space that was his office by the front
door of this apartment block.

'Stay here. I'll fetch those bikes from the
basement. Could do with checkin' that the rub-
bish has been collected.'

'Oh, thanks, Jack.' It was always a mission
managing two small boys and their bikes in the
elevator. This way, he could get their coats and
helmets securely fastened without them trying
to climb on board their beloved bikes.

As always, he cast more than one glance
towards the door at the back of the foyer as
he got ready to head outside. He remembered

wanting to knock on it when Grace had first moved in and that he'd been held back by some nebulous idea of boundaries. He didn't have any problems with it now.

They'd come a long way since then. Too far, perhaps, but they'd obviously both decided to put that ill-advised kiss behind them and focus on a friendship that was growing steadily stronger.

And Charles had news that he really wanted to share.

So he knocked on Grace's door. He knew she had a day off today because he'd started taking more notice of her name on the weekly rosters.

'Charles… Hi…' Was it his imagination or was there a glow of real pleasure amidst the surprise of a morning caller?

He could certainly feel that glow but maybe it was coming from his own pleasure at seeing *her*. Especially away from work, when she wasn't wearing her scrubs, with her hair scraped back from her face in her usual ponytail. Today, she was in jeans tucked into sheepskin-lined boots and she had a bright red sweater and her hair was falling around her face in messy waves—a bit like it had been when he'd come home to find her sound asleep on his couch.

Horse sneaked past her legs and made a bee-line for the boys, who shrieked with glee and fell on their furry friend for cuddles.

'I have something I have to tell you,' Charles said.

Her eyes widened. 'Oh, no...is it Miranda? Helena texted me to say she was involved in that subway tunnel collapse—that she'd been trapped under rubble or something.'

Charles shook his head. 'She's fine. She didn't even need to come into the ER. A para-medic took care of her, apparently. No, it's about Toby. I just had a call from PICU.'

He could hear the gasp as Grace sucked in her breath. 'Toby?'

'Yes. He woke up this morning.'

'Oh...it's been forty-eight hours. I was start-ing to think the worst... Is he...? Has he...?'

'As far as they can tell, he's neurologically intact. They're going to run more tests but he recognises his parents and he's said the few words he knows. And he's smiling...'

Grace was smiling, too. Beaming, in fact. And then she noticed Jack as the elevator doors opened and he stepped out with a small bike under each arm.

'Morning, Jack.'

'Morning, Miss Forbes.' His face broke into a wide grin. 'Yo' sure look happy today.'

'I am…' There was a sparkle in her eyes that looked like unshed tears as she met Charles's gaze again. 'So happy. Thanks so much for coming to tell me.'

'Can Horse come to the park?' Max was beside his father's legs. 'Can he watch us ride our bikes?'

The glance from Grace held a query now. Did Charles want their company?

He smiled. Of course he did.

'Wrap up warm,' Jack warned. 'It's only about five degrees out there. It might snow.'

'Really?' Grace sounded excited. 'I can't wait for it to snow. And I'm really, really hoping for a white Christmas this year.'

'Could happen.' Jack nodded. 'They're predicting some big storms for December and that's not far off. It'll be Christmas before we know it.'

Charles groaned. 'Let's get Thanksgiving out of the way before we start talking Christmas. We've only just finished Halloween!'

Except Halloween felt like a long way in the past now, didn't it? Long enough for this friendship to feel like it was becoming something much more solid.

Real.

'Give me two minutes,' Grace said. 'I need to find my hat and scarf. Horse? Come and get your harness on.'

The boys had trainer wheels on their small bikes and needed constant reminding not to get too far ahead of the adults. Pedestrians on the busy pavement had to jump out of the way as the boys powered towards the park but most of them smiled at the two identical little faces with their proud smiles. Charles kept a firm hand on each set of handlebars as they crossed the main road at the lights but once they were through the gates of Central Park, he let them go as fast as they wanted.

'Phew...I think we're safe now. I'm pretty sure the tourist carriages don't use this path.'

'Do they do sleigh rides here when it snows?'

'I don't know. I've seen carriages that look like sleighs but I think they have wheels rather than runners. Why?'

Grace's breath came out in a huff of white as she sighed. 'It's always been my dream for Christmas. A sleigh ride in a snowy park. At night, when there's sparkly lights everywhere and there are bells on the horses and you have to be all wrapped up in soft blankets.'

Charles smiled but he felt a squeeze of something poignant catch his heart. The picture she was painting was ultimately romantic but did she see herself alone in that sleigh?

He couldn't ask. They might have reached new ground with their friendship, especially after that oddly intimate case of working to save little Toby, but asking such a personal question seemed premature. Risky.

Besides, Grace was still talking.

'Christmas in Australia was so weird. Too hot to do anything but head for the nearest beach or pool but lots of people still want to do the whole roast turkey thing. Or dress up in Santa suits.' She rubbed at her nose, which was already red from the cold. 'It feels much more like a proper Christmas when it snows.'

The boys were turning their bikes in a circle ahead of them, which seemed to be a complicated procedure. And then they were pedalling furiously back towards them.

'Look at us, Gace! Look how fast we can go.'

Grace leapt out of Cameron's way, pulling Houston to safety as Cameron tried, and failed, to slow down. The bike tilted sideways and then toppled.

'Whoops...' Charles scooped up his son. 'Okay, buddy?'

Cameron's face crumpled but then he sniffed hard and nodded.

'Is it time for a hotdog?'

'Soon.' He was climbing back onto his bike. 'I have to ride some more first.'

'He's determined,' Grace said, watching him pedal after his brother. 'Like his daddy.'

'Oh? You think I'm determined?'

'Absolutely. You don't give up easily, even if you have a challenge that would defeat a lot of people.'

'You mean Toby? You were just as determined as I was to save him.'

'Mmm. But I'd seen that look in your eyes before, remember? I'm not sure if I would have had the confidence to try that hard when I had absolutely no experience, like you did back when we were students.' She shook her head. 'I still don't have that much experience of arrest from hypothermia. That old woman that we worked on is the only other case I've ever had. Bit of a coincidence, isn't it?'

'Meant to be,' Charles suggested lightly. 'We're a good team.'

'It's easier to be determined when you're part of a team,' Grace said quietly. 'I think you've coped amazingly with challenges you've had to face alone. Your boys are a credit to you.'

He might not know her story yet but he knew that Grace had been through her own share of tough challenges.

He spoke quietly as well. 'I have a feeling you've done that, too.'

The glance they shared acknowledged the truth. And their connection. A mutual appreciation of another person's strength of character, perhaps?

And Charles was quite sure that Grace was almost ready to tell him what he wanted to know. That all it would take was the right question. But he had no idea what that question might be and this was hardly the best place to start a conversation that needed care. He could feel the cold seeping through his shoes and gloves and he would need to take the boys home soon.

'Come and visit later, if you're not busy,' he found himself suggesting. 'The boys got a train set from my parents for their birthday and they'd love to show it to you.'

The twins were on the return leg of one of

the loops that took them away from their father and then back again.

'What do you think, Max?' he called out. 'Is it a good idea for Grace to come and see your new train?'

Later, Charles knew he would feel a little guilty about enlisting his sons' backup like this but right then, he just wanted to know that he was going to get to spend some more time with Grace.

Soon.

It seemed important.

'*Yes*,' Max shouted obligingly, his instant grin an irresistible invitation. 'And Horse.'

'And mac and cheese,' Cameron added.

But Max shook his head. 'Not Daddy's,' he said sadly. 'It comes in a box. I don't like it…'

Charles raised an eyebrow. 'This is your fault, Grace. I have at least half a dozen boxes of Easy Mac 'n' Cheese in my pantry—my go-to quick favourite dinner for the boys—and they're useless. Even when I try adding bacon.'

'Oh, dear…' Grace was smiling. 'Guess I'd better teach you how to make cheese sauce, then?'

His nod was solemn. 'I think so. You did promise.'

Her cheeks were already pink from the cold

but Charles had the impression that the colour had deepened even more suddenly.

'I think I promised to write it down for you.'

'Ah…but I learn so much better by doing something. Do you remember that class we did on suturing once? When we had that pig skin to practise on?'

'Yes… It was fun.'

'Tricky, though. I'd stayed up the night before, reading all about exactly where to grasp a needle with the needle driver and wrapping the suture around it and then switching hand positions to make the knots. I even watched a whole bunch of videos.'

'Ha! I knew you always stayed up all night studying. It was why I had so much trouble keeping up with you.'

'My point is, actually doing it was a completely different story. I felt like I had two left hands. You were way better at it.'

'Not by the end of the class. You aced it.'

'Because I was doing it. Not reading about it, or watching it.'

Why was he working so hard to persuade her to do something that she might not be comfortable with? Because it felt important—just like the idea of spending more time with her?

There was something about the way her

gaze slid away from his that made him want to touch her arm. To tell her that this was okay. That she could trust him.

But maybe he managed to communicate that, anyway, in the briefest glance she returned to, because her breath came out in a cloudy puff again—the way it had when she'd sighed after confessing her dream of having a Christmas sleigh ride in the snow. Her chin bobbed in a single nod.

'I'll pick up some ingredients on my way home.'

'We don't want to go home, Daddy,' Cameron said. 'We want to go to the playground.'

With their determined pedalling efforts, their feet probably weren't as cold as his, Charles decided. And with some running and climbing added in, they were going to be very tired by this evening. They'd probably fall asleep as soon as they'd had their dinner and...and that would be the perfect opportunity to talk to Grace, wouldn't it?

Really talk to Grace.

He smiled at his boys. 'Okay. Let's head for the playground.'

'And Gace,' Max added.

But she shook her head. 'I can't, sorry, sweetheart. I have to take Horse home now.'

'Why?'

'Because Stefan and Jerome are going to Skype us and talk to him, like they do every Sunday. And he needs his hair brushed first. Oh…I've just had an idea.' She held the dog's lead out to Charles. 'Can you stand with the boys? I'll take a photo I can send them, so they can see that he's been having fun in the park today.'

It took a moment or two to get two small boys, two bikes, a large fluffy dog and a tall man into a cohesive enough group to photograph. And then a passer-by stopped and insisted on taking the phone from Grace's hands.

'You need one of the whole family,' he said firmly.

Grace looked startled. And then embarrassed as she caught Charles's gaze.

It reminded him of Davenport family photos. Where everyone had to look as though they were a happy family and hide the undercurrents and secret emotions that were too private to share. The kind of image that would be taken very soon for their annual Thanksgiving gathering?

Charles was good at this. He'd been doing it for a very long time. And he knew it was far easier to just get it over with than try and explain why it wasn't a good idea.

So he smiled at Grace and pulled Houston a bit closer to make a space for her to stand beside him, behind the boys on their bikes.

'Come on,' he encouraged. 'Before we all freeze to death here.'

Strangely, when Grace was in place a moment later, with Charles's arm draped over her shoulders, it didn't feel at all like the uncomfortable publicity shots of the New York Davenports destined to appear in some glossy magazine.

It was, in fact, surprisingly easy to find the 'big smile' that the stranger requested.

It wasn't a case of her heart conflicting with her head, which would have been far simpler to deal with.

This was more like her heart arranging itself into two separate divisions on either side of what was more like a solid wall than a battle line.

There were moments when Grace could even believe there was a door hidden in that wall, somewhere, and time with Charles felt like she was moving along, tapping on that solid surface, waiting for the change in sound that would tell her she was close.

Moments like this, as she stood beside Charles in his kitchen, supervising his first attempt at making a cheese sauce.

'Add the milk gradually and just keep stirring.'

'It's all lumpy.'

'It'll be fine. Stir a bit faster. And have faith.'

'Hmm…okay…' Charles peered into the pot, frowning. 'How did your Skype session go?'

'Houston wasn't terribly co-operative. He didn't want to wake up. I showed them the photo from the park, though, and they said to say "hi" and wish you a happy Thanksgiving.'

'That's nice.' Charles added some more milk to his sauce. 'Where are they going to be celebrating? Still in Italy?'

'Yes. They're fallen head over heels in love with the Amalfi coast. They've bought a house there.'

'What? How's that going to work?'

'They've got this idea that they could spend six months in Europe and six months here every year and never have winters.'

'But what about Houston?'

'I guess he'll have to get used to travelling.' Grace pointed at the pot. 'Keep stirring or lumps will sneak in. You can add the grated cheese now, too.'

Charles was shaking his head. 'I don't think Houston would like summers in Italy. It'd be too hot for a big, fluffy dog.'

'Mmm...' Grace looked over her shoulder. Not that she could see into the living area from here but she could imagine that Houston hadn't moved from where the boys had commanded him to stay—a canine mountain that they were constructing a new train line around. From the happy tooting noises she could hear, it seemed like the line was up and running now.

'I'd adopt him,' Charles said. 'Max and Cameron think he's another brother.'

'I would, too.' Grace smiled. 'I love that dog. I don't think you ever feel truly lonely when you're sharing your life with a dog.'

The glance from Charles was quick enough to be sharp. A flash of surprise followed by something very warm, like sympathy. Concern...

She was stepping onto dangerous territory here, inadvertently admitting that she was often lonely.

'Right...let's drain that pasta, mix in the bacon and you can pour the sauce over the top. All we need is the breadcrumbs on top with a bit more cheese and it can go in the oven for half an hour.'

The distraction seemed to have been successful and Grace relaxed again, helping herself to a glass of wine when Charles chased the boys into the bathroom to get clean. She had to abandon her drink before their dinner was ready to come out of the oven, though, in order to answer the summons to the bathroom where she found Charles kneeling beside a huge tub that contained two small boys, a flotilla of plastic toys and a ridiculous amount of bubbles.

'Look, Gace. A snowman!'

'Could be a snow woman,' Charles suggested. 'Or possibly a snow dog.'

He had taken off the ribbed, navy pullover he'd been wearing and his T-shirt had large, damp patches on the front. There were clumps of bubbles on his bare arms and another one on the top of his head and the grin on his face told her that, in this moment, Charles Davenport was possibly the happiest man on earth.

Tap, tap, tap...

Would she be brave enough to go through that door if she *did* find it?

What if she opened her heart to this little

family and then found they didn't actually want her?

'Nobody's ever going to want you again... Not now...'

That ugly voice from the past should have lost its power long ago but there were still moments. Like this one, when she was smiling down at two, perfect, beautiful children and a man that she knew was even more gorgeous without those designer jeans and shirt.

Even as her smile began to wobble, though, she was saved by the bell of the oven timer.

'I'll take that out,' she excused herself. 'Dinner will be ready by the time you guys have got your jimjams on.'

The twins were just as cute in their pyjamas as they had been in their monkey suits for Halloween but another glass of wine had made it easier for Grace. The pleasant fuzziness reminded her that it was possible to embrace the moment and enjoy this for simply what it was—spending time with a friend and being included in his family.

Because they were real friends now, with a shared history of good times in the past and an understanding of how hard it could be to move on from tougher aspects in life. Maybe that kiss had let them both know that anything other than friendship would be a mistake. It was weeks ago and there had been no hint of anything more than a growing trust.

Look at them…having a relaxed dinner in front of a fire, with an episode of *Curious George* on the television and a contented dog stretched out on the mat, and the might-have-beens weren't trying to break her heart. Grace was loving every minute of it.

Okay, it was a bit harder when she got the sleepy cuddles and kisses from the boys before Charles carried them off to bed but even then she wasn't in any hurry to escape. This time, she wasn't going to go home until she had cleaned up the kitchen. She wasn't even going to get off this couch until she had finished this particularly delicious glass of wine.

And then Charles came back and sat on the couch beside her and everything suddenly seemed even more delicious.

Tap, tap, tap…

For a heartbeat, Grace could actually hear the sound. Because the expression on Charles's face made her wonder if he was tapping at a wall of his own?

Maybe it was her own heartbeat she could hear as it picked up its pace.

He hadn't forgotten that comment about being lonely at all, had he?

'Have you got any plans for Thanksgiving tomorrow, Grace? You'd be welcome to join us, although a full-on Davenport occasion might be a bit…' He made a face that suggested he wasn't particularly looking forward to it himself. 'Sorry, I shouldn't make assumptions. You've probably got your own family to think about.'

Her own family. A separate family. That wall had just got a lot more solid.

Grace didn't protest when Charles refilled her glass.

'I had thought of going to visit my dad but I would have had to find someone to care for Houston and I didn't have enough of a gap in my roster. It's a long way to go just for a night or two. He might come to New York for Christmas, though.'

'And you lost your mum, didn't you? I remember you telling me how much you missed her.'

Good grief…he actually remembered what she'd said that night when she'd been crying on his shoulder as a result of her stress about her final exams?

'She died a couple of years before I went to med school. Ovarian cancer.'

'Oh…that must have been tough.'

'Yeah…it was. Dad's never got over it.' Grace fell silent. Had she just reminded Charles of his own loss. That he would never get over it?

The silence stretched long enough for Charles to finish his glass of wine and refill it.

'There's something else I should apologise for, too.'

'What?' Grace tried to lighten what felt like an oddly serious vibe. Was he going to apologise for that kiss? Explain why it had been such a mistake? 'You're going to send me into the kitchen to do the dishes?'

He wasn't smiling.

'I treated you badly,' he said quietly. 'Back in med school. After…that night…'

Oh, help… This was breaking the first rule in the new book. The one that made that night a taboo subject.

'I don't know how much you knew of what hit the fan the next day regarding the Davenport scandal…'

'Not much,' Grace confessed. 'I heard about it, of course, but I was a bit preoccupied. With, you know…finals coming up.'

And dealing with the rejection…

He nodded. 'The pressure was intense, wasn't it? And I was trying to stop my family completely disintegrating. The intrusion of the media was unbelievable. They ripped my father to shreds, which only made us all more aware of how damaged our own relationship with him was. It tarnished all the good memories we had as a family. It nearly destroyed us.

'We'd always been in the limelight as one of the most important families in New York,' he continued quietly. 'A perfect family. And then it turns out that my father had been living a lie. That he'd had an affair. That there was a half-sister none of us knew about.'

He cleared his throat. 'I was the oldest and it was down to me to handle the media and focus on what mattered and the only way I could do that was to ignore how *I* felt. My only job was to protect the people that mattered most to me and, at that time, it had to be my family. It hit my mother hardest, as you can probably imagine, but they went to town on Miranda's mother, too. Describing her as worthless was one of the kinder labels. I didn't know her and I probably wouldn't have wanted to but I did know that my new half-sister was just a scared kid who had nobody to protect her. She was as vulnerable as you could get...'

Grace bit her lip. Charles couldn't help himself, could he? He had to protect the vulnerable. It had been the reason why they'd been together that night—he'd felt the need to protect *her*. To comfort her. To make her feel strong enough to cope with the world.

That ability to care for others more than himself was a huge part of what made him such an amazing person.

And, yes...she could understand why his attention had been so convincingly distracted.

Could forgive it, even?

'By the time things settled down, you were gone.'

Grace shrugged. Of course she had gone. There had been nothing to stay for. Would it have changed things if she'd known how difficult life was for Charles at that time?

Maybe.

Or maybe not. It was more likely that she would have been made much more aware of how different his world was and how unlikely it would have been that she could have been a part of it.

'I can't imagine what it must have been like. Life can be difficult enough without having your privacy invaded like that. I couldn't think of anything worse...' Grace shook her head. 'I get that a one-night stand would have fallen off your radar. You don't need to apologise.'

But it was nice that he had.

'It was a lot more than a one-night stand, Grace.' The words were quiet. Convincing. 'You need to know that. And I asked about you, later—every time I came across someone from school at a conference or something. That was how I found out you'd got married.'

Grace was silent. He'd been asking about her? Looking for her, even? If she had known that, would she have taken her relationship with Mike as far as marrying him?

Possibly not. She had thought she'd found love but she'd always known the connection hadn't been as fierce as the one she'd found with Charles that night.

'It was just after that that I met Nina,' he continued. There was a hint of a smile tugging at his lips. 'Even then, I thought, well...if you could get married and live happily ever after, I'd better make sure I didn't get left behind.'

The silence was very poignant this time.

'I'm sorry,' Grace whispered. 'Everybody knows how much you loved her. I'm so sorry you didn't get your happily ever after.'

'I got some wonderful memories. And two amazing children. You reminded me just how lucky I am, on your first day at work.' Charles drew in a deep breath and let it out slowly. 'I hope you have things to feel lucky about, too.'

'Of course I do.'

'Like?'

Grace swallowed hard. She was leaning against that wall in her heart now, as if she needed support to stay upright.

But maybe she needed more than that. To hear someone agree that she was lucky?

'I'm alive,' she whispered.

She could feel his shock. Did he think she was making a reference to Nina? Grace closed her eyes. She hadn't intended saying more but she couldn't leave it like that.

'I found a lump in my breast,' she said slowly, into the silence. 'I'd been married for about a year by then and Mike was keen to start a family. The lump turned out to be only a cyst but, because of my mother, they ran a lot of tests and one of them was for the genetic markers that let you know how much risk you have of getting ovarian or breast cancer. Mine was as high as it gets. And some people think that pregnancy can make that worse.'

'So you decided not to have kids?'

Grace shook her head, glancing up. 'No. I decided I'd have them as quickly as possible and then have a hysterectomy and mastectomy. Only…it didn't work out that way because they found another lump and that one wasn't a cyst. So…I decided to get the surgery and give up any dreams of having kids.'

She had to close her eyes again. 'Mike couldn't handle that. And he couldn't handle the treatment—especially the chemo and living with someone who was sick all the time. And later, my scars were just a reminder of what I'd taken away from him. A mother for his children. A woman he could look at without being…' her next word came out like a tiny sob '…disgusted…'

Maybe she had known how Charles would react.

Maybe she had wanted, more than anything, to feel his arms around her, like this.

To hear his voice, soft against her ear.

'You're gorgeous, Grace. There are no scars that could ever take that away.'

She could hear the steady thump of his heart and feel the solid comfort of the band of his arms around her.

'You're strong, too. I fought external things and I'm not sure that I did such a great job but you…you fought a battle that you could never step away from, even for a moment. And you won.'

Grace's breath caught in a hitch. She *had* won. She would never forget any one of those steps towards hearing those magic words…

Cancer-free…

'Your courage blows me away,' Charles continued. 'You not only got through that battle with the kind of obstacles that your jerk of a husband added but you took yourself off to work in places that are as tough as they get. You didn't let it dent your sense of adventure or the amazing ability you have to care for others.' His arms tightened around her. 'You should be so proud of yourself. Don't ever let anything that he said or did take any of that away from you.'

Grace had to look up. To make sure that his eyes were telling her the same thing that his words were. To see if what she was feeling right now was something real. That she could be proud of everything she'd been through. That she could, finally, dismiss the legacy that Mike's rejection had engraved on her soul. That she was so much stronger now…

How amazing was this that Charles could

make her feel as if she'd just taken the biggest step ever into a bright, new future?

That she'd found someone who made it possible to take the kind of risk that she'd never believed she would be strong enough to take again?

And maybe she had known what would happen when they fell into each other's eyes again like this.

As the distance between them slowly disappeared and their lips touched.

That door in the wall in her heart had been so well hidden she hadn't even realised she was leaning right against it until it fell open with their combined weight.

And the other side was a magic place where scars didn't matter.

Where they could be touched by someone else. Kissed, even, and it wasn't shameful. Or terrifying.

It was real. Raw. And heartbreakingly beautiful.

No. It wasn't 'someone else' who could have done this.

It could only have been Charles.

CHAPTER EIGHT

THE SOFT TRILL advertising an incoming text message on his phone woke Charles.

It could have been from anyone. One of his siblings, perhaps. Or a message from work to warn him that there was a situation requiring his input.

But he knew it was from Grace.

He just *knew*…

And, in that moment of knowing, there was a profound pleasure. Excitement, even. An instant pull back into the astonishing connection they had rediscovered last night that was still hovering at the edges of his consciousness as he reached sleepily for the phone on his bedside table.

Okay, he'd broken rule number one, not only by allowing female companionship to progress to this level but by allowing it to happen under his own roof and not keeping it totally separate from his home life—and his children.

And he'd broken an even bigger, albeit undefined, rule, by doing it with someone that he had a potentially important emotional connection to.

Had he been blindsided, because that connection had already been there and only waiting to be uncovered and that meant he hadn't been able to make a conscious choice to back off before it was even a possibility?

Maybe his undoing had been the way her story had touched his heart. That someone as clever and warm and beautiful as Grace could have been made to believe that she didn't deserve to be loved.

Whatever had pushed him past his boundaries, it had felt inevitable by the time he'd led Grace to his bed. And everything that had happened after that was a blurred mix of sensation and emotion that was overwhelming, even now.

Physically, it had been as astonishing as that first time. Exquisite. But there had been more to it this time. So much more. The gift of trust that she'd given him. The feeling that the dark place in his soul had been flooded with a light he'd never expected to experience again after

Nina had died. Had never wanted to experience again because he knew what it was like when it got turned off?

It was early, with only the faintest suggestion of the approaching day between the gap of curtains that had been hastily pulled. Grace would be at work already, though. Her early shift had been the reason she hadn't stayed all night and Charles hadn't tried to persuade her. The twins might be far too young to read anything into finding Grace and Horse in their apartment first thing in the morning but what if they dropped an innocent bombshell in front of their grandparents, for instance, during the family's Thanksgiving dinner tonight?

He wasn't ready to share any of this.

It was too new—this feeling of an intimate connection, when you could get a burst of pleasure from even the prospect of communication via text.

He wasn't exactly sure how he felt about it himself yet, so he certainly didn't want the opinions of anyone else—like his parents or his siblings. This was very private.

There was only one other person on the planet who could share this.

Can't believe I left without doing the dishes again. I owe you one. xx

For a moment Charles let his head sink into his pillow again, a smile spreading over his face. He loved Grace's humour. And how powerful two little letters could be at the end of a message. Not one kiss, but two…

Powerful letters.

Even more powerful feelings.

They reminded him of the heady days of falling in love with Nina, when they couldn't bear to be apart. When they were the only two people in the world that mattered.

Was that what was happening here?

Was he falling in *love* with Grace?

His smile faded. The swirling potentially humorous responses to her text message vanished. He'd known that he would never fall in love again. He'd known that from the moment Nina's life had ebbed away that terrible day and he hadn't given it a second thought since. That part of his life had simply been dismissed as he'd coped with what had been important. His babies. And his work.

It had been a very long time before his body reminded him that there were other needs that could be deemed of importance. That was when rule number one had been considered and then put into place.

And he'd broken it.

Without giving any thought to any implications.

The jarring sound of his phone starting to ring cut through the heavy thoughts pressing down and suffocating the pleasure of any memories of last night. His heart skipped a beat with what felt like alarm as he glanced at the screen.

But it wasn't Grace calling. It was his mother.

At this time of the day?

'Mom…what's up? Is everything all right?'

'Maybe you can tell me, Charles. Who is she?'

'Sorry?'

'I'm reading the *New York Post*. Page six…'

Of course she was. Anyone who was anyone in New York turned to page six first, either to read about someone they knew or about themselves. It was a prime example of the gossip columns that Charles hated above everything else. The kind that had almost destroyed his family once as people fed on every juicy detail that the Davenport scandal had offered. The kind that had made getting through the tragedy of losing his wife just that much harder as the details of their fairy-tale romance and wedding were pored over again. The kind that had made him keep his own life as private as possible ever since in his determination to protect his sons.

'Why now?' Vanessa continued. 'Really, Charles. We could do without another airing of the family's dirty laundry. Especially today, with it being Thanksgiving.'

He was out of bed now, clad only in his pyjama pants as he headed into the living area. His laptop was on the dining table, already open. It took only a couple of clicks to find what his mother was referring to.

The photograph was a shock. How on earth had a journalist got hold of it when it had been taken only yesterday—on Grace's phone?

But there it was. The boys on their bikes on either side of Houston. Himself with his arm slung over Grace's shoulders. And they were all grinning like the archetypal happy family.

His brain was working overtime. Had that friendly stranger actually been a journalist? Or had Grace shared the photograph on social media? No... But she had shared it with Stefan and Jerome and they had many friends who were the kind of celebrities that often graced page six. Easy pickings for anyone who contributed to this gossip column, thanks to a thoughtless moment on his behalf.

'She's a friend, Mom. Someone I went to med school with, who happens to be living downstairs at the moment. Dog-sitting.'

'That's not what's getting assumed.'

'Of course it isn't. Why do you even read this stuff?'

He scanned the headline.

Who is the mystery woman in Charles Davenport's life?

'And why are they raking over old news? It's too much. Really, Charles. Can't you be more careful?'

Speed-reading was a skill he had mastered a long time ago.

It's been a while since we caught up with the New York Davenports. Who could forget the scandal of the love child that almost blew this famous family apart? Where is she now, you might be asking? Where are any of them, in fact?

Moving on with their lives, apparently. Dr Charles Davenport is retired, with his notoriously private firstborn son taking over as chief of the ER at Manhattan Mercy in the manner of the best dynasties. He's become something of a recluse since the tragic death of his wife but it looks as though he's finally moving on. And isn't it a treat to get a peek at his adorable twin sons?

We see his own twin brother Elijah more than any of the family members, with his penchant for attending every important party, and with a different woman on his arm every time. Their sister Penelope is a celebrated daredevil and the youngest brother, Zachary, is reportedly returning to the family fold very soon, in more ways than one. He has resigned from the Navy and will be adding his medical skills to the Davenport team at Manhattan Mercy. Watch this space for more news later.

And the love child, Miranda? Well... she's so much a part of the family now she's also a doctor and it's no surprise that she's working in exactly the same place.

Are the New York Davenports an example of what doesn't kill you makes you stronger? Or is it just window dressing...?

Charles stopped reading as the article went on to focus on Vanessa Davenport's recent philanthropic endeavours. His mother was still talking—about a fundraising luncheon she was supposed to be attending in a matter of hours.

'How can I go? There'll be reporters everywhere and intrusive questions. But, if I don't go, it'll just fuel speculation. *Everybody* will be talking about it.'

'Just ignore it,' Charles advised. 'Keep your head high, smile and say "No comment". It'll die down. It always does.'

He could hear the weary sigh on the other end of the line.

'I'm so sick of it. We've all been through enough. Haven't we?'

'Mmm.' Charles rubbed his forehead with his fingers. 'I have to go, Mom. The boys are waking up and we need to get ready. It's the Macy's Thanksgiving parade today and we'll have to get there early to find a good place to watch. I'll see you tonight.'

It should have been such a happy day.

Some of Charles's earliest memories were of the sheer wonder of this famous parade. Of being in a privileged viewing position with his siblings, bundled up against the cold, jumping up and down with the amazement of every new sight and adding his own contribution to the cacophony of sound—the music and cheers and squeals of excitement—that built and built until the finale they were all waiting for when Santa Claus in his sleigh being pulled by reindeer with spectacular gilded antlers would let them know that the excitement wasn't over. Christmas was coming...

This was the first year that Cameron and Max were old enough to appreciate the spectacle and not be frightened by the crowds and noise. They were well bundled up in their coats and mittens and hats and their little faces were shining with excitement. They found a spot on Central Park West, not far from one of their favourite playgrounds, and Charles held a twin on each hip, giving them a clear view over the older children in front of them.

The towering balloons sailed past. Superman and Spiderman and Muppets and Disney characters. There was a brass band with its members dressed like tin soldiers and people on stilts that looked like enormous candy canes with their striped costumes and the handles on their tall hats. There were clowns and jugglers and dancers and they kept coming.

Charles's arms began to ache with the weight of the twins and their joyous wriggling.

He wasn't going to put them down. This was his job. Supporting his boys. Protecting them. And he could cope. The three of them would always cope. The happiness that today should have provided was clouded for Charles, though. He could feel an echo that reminded him of his mother's heavy sigh earlier this morning.

That it was starting again. The media interest that could become like a searchlight, illuminating so many things that were best left in the shade now. Things that were nobody else's business. Putting them out there for others to speculate on only made things so much harder to deal with.

He could still feel the pain of photographs that had been put on public display in the aftermath of the family scandal breaking. Of the snippets of gossip, whether true or not, that had been raked over. The fresh wave of interest in the days after Nina's death had been even worse as he'd struggled to deal with his own grief. Seeing that photograph that had been taken at their engagement party, with Nina looking so stunning in her white designer gown, proudly showing off the famed Davenport, pink diamond ring, had been like a kick in the guts.

What if that photograph surfaced again now, with gossip mills cranking up at the notion that he'd found a new partner? Grace was nothing like Nina, who'd been part of the kind of society he'd grown up in. Nina had been well used to being in the public eye. Grace was someone who kept herself in the background, working as part of a team in her job where the centre stage was always taken by the person needing her help.

Or making two small boys happy by baking cookies and trashing his kitchen...

She would be appalled at any media interest. She'd as much as told him how she wouldn't be able to cope.

'I can't imagine what it must have been like. Life can be difficult enough without having your privacy invaded like that. I couldn't think of anything worse...'

The cloud settled even more heavily over Charles as the real implications hit him.

He knew her story now. That she had been broken by the reaction of the man who had been her husband to the battle she'd had to fight. That she'd actually hidden herself from the world to come to terms with being made to feel less than loveable. Ugly, even...

He hadn't even noticed her scars last night. Not as anything that detracted from her beauty, anyway. If anything, they added to it because they were a mark of her astonishing courage and strength.

But he knew exactly how vulnerable she could still be, despite that strength.

As vulnerable as his younger siblings had been when the 'love child' scandal had broken. He'd learned how to shut things down then, in order to protect them.

Maybe he needed to call on those skills again now.

To protect Grace. He could imagine the devastating effect if the spotlight was turned on her. If someone thought to find images of what mastectomy scars looked like, perhaps, and coupled it with headline bait like *Is this why her husband left her?*

He couldn't let that happen.

He *wouldn't* let that happen.

He had to protect his boys, too.

They weren't just old enough to appreciate this parade now. They knew—and loved— the new person who had come into their lives. Someone who was as happy as he was to stand in the cold and watch them run and climb in a playground. Who baked cookies with them and fell asleep on the couch with them cuddled beside her.

He wouldn't be the only one to be left with a dark place if she vanished from their lives.

What about that different perspective he'd found the day after the twins' birthday, when he'd known that he wouldn't want his boys growing up without a dad, if the tragedy had been reversed? That he wouldn't have wanted Nina to have a restricted, celibate life?

It was all spiralling out of control. His feelings for Grace. How close they had suddenly become. The threat of having his private life picked over by emotional vultures, thanks to media interest and having important things damaged beyond repair.

Yes. He needed to remember lessons learned. That control could be regained eventually if things could be ignored. He had done this before but this time he could do it better. He was responsible and he was old enough and wise enough this time around not to make the same mistakes.

He had to choose each step with great care. And the first step was to narrow his focus to what was most important.

And he was holding that in his arms.

'Show's almost over, guys. Want to go to the playground on the way home?'

'There's something different about you today.' Helena looked up as she finished scribbling a note in a patient file on the main desk in the ER. 'You look...happy.'

Grace's huff was indignant. 'Are you trying to tell me I usually look miserable?'

'No...' Helena was smiling but she still had a puzzled frown. 'You never look *miserable*. You just don't usually look...I don't know... *this* happy. Not at this time of the morning, anyway.'

Grace shrugged but found herself averting her gaze in case her friend might actually see more than she was ready to share.

She'd already seen too much.

This happiness was seeping out of every cell in her body and it was no surprise it was visible to someone who knew her well. It felt like she was glowing. As if she could still feel the touch of Charles's hands—and lips—on her body.

On more than her body, in fact. It felt like her soul was glowing this morning.

Reborn.

Oh, help... She wasn't going to be as focused on her work today as she needed to be if she let herself get pulled back into memories of last night. That was a pleasure that needed to wait until later. With a huge effort, Grace closed the mental door on that compelling space.

'I have a clown in Curtain Three,' she told Helena.

Helena shook her head with a grimace. 'We get a lot of clowns in here. They're usually drunk.'

'No...this is a real clown. He was trying to do a cartwheel and I've just finished relocating his shoulder that couldn't cope. I want to check his X-ray before I discharge him. He has a clown friend with him, too. Didn't you see them come in? Spotty suits, squeaky horns, bright red wigs—the whole works.'

But Helena didn't seem to be listening. She was staring at an ambulance gurney that was being wheeled past the desk. The person lying on the gurney seemed to be a life-sized tin soldier.

'Oh...of course...' she sighed. 'It's the Macy's Thanksgiving parade today, isn't it?'

'Chest pain,' one of the paramedics announced. 'Query ST elevation in the inferior leads.'

'Straight into Resus, thanks.' Grace shared a glance with Helena. This tin soldier was probably having a heart attack. 'I can take this.'

Helena nodded. 'I'll follow up on your clown, if you like.' She glanced over her shoulder as if she was expecting more gurneys to be rolling up. 'We're in for a crazy day,' she murmured. 'It always is, with the parade.'

Crazy was probably good, Grace decided as she followed her tin soldier into Resus.

'Let's get him onto the bed. On my count. One, two…*three*.' She smiled at the middle-aged man. 'My name's Grace and I'm one of the doctors here at Manhattan Mercy. Don't worry, we're going to take good care of you. What's your name?'

'Tom.'

'How old are you, Tom?'

'Fifty-three.'

'Do you have any medical history of heart problems? Hypertension? Diabetes?'

Tom was shaking his head to every query.

'Have you ever had chest pain like this before?'

Another shake. 'I get a bit out of puff sometimes. But playing the trumpet is hard, you know?'

'And you got out of breath this morning?'

'Yeah. And then I felt sick and got real sweaty. And the pain...'

'He's had six milligrams of morphine.' A paramedic was busy helping the nursing staff to change the leads that clipped to the electrodes dotting Tom's chest so that he was attached to the hospital's monitor. His oxygen tubing came off the portable cylinder to be linked to the overhead supply and a different blood pressure cuff was being wrapped around his arm.

'How's the pain now, Tom?' Grace asked. 'On a scale of zero to ten, with ten being the worst?'

'About six, I guess.'

'It was ten when we got to him.'

'Let's give you a bit more pain relief, then,' Grace said. 'And I want some bloods off for cardiac enzymes, please. I want a twelve-lead ECG, stat. And can someone call the cath lab and check availability?'

Yes. Crazy was definitely good. From the moment Tom had arrived in her care to nearly an hour later, when she accompanied him to the cardiac catheter laboratory so that he could receive angioplasty to open his blocked artery, she didn't have a spare second where her thoughts could travel to where they wanted to go so much.

Heading back to the ER was a different matter.

Her route that took her back to bypass the main waiting area was familiar now. The medical staff all used it because if you went through the waiting area at busy times, you ran the risk of being confronted by angry people who didn't like the fact that they had to wait while more urgent cases were prioritised. If Helena was right, this was going to be a very busy day. Which made sense, because they were the closest hospital to where the parade was happening and the participants and spectators would number in the tens of thousands.

Had Charles taken the boys to see the parade?

Was that why he hadn't had the time to answer her text message yet?

Grace's hand touched the phone that was clipped to the waistband of her scrub trousers but she resisted the urge to bring the screen to life and check that she hadn't missed a message.

She wasn't some love-crazed teenager who was holding her breath to hear from a boy.

She'd never been that girl. Had never dated a boy that had had that much of an impact on her. She'd been confident in her life choices and her focus on her study and the career she wanted more than anything.

But she'd turned into that girl, hadn't she? After that first night with Charles Davenport. The waiting for that message or call. The excitement that had morphed into anxiety and then crushing disappointment and heartbreak.

And humiliation...

Grace dropped her hand. They were a long way from being teenagers now. Charles was a busy man. Quite apart from his job, he was a hands-on father with two small boys. History was not about to repeat itself. Charles understood how badly he had treated her by ignoring her last time. He had apologised for it, even. There was no way he would do that again.

And she was stronger. He'd told her that. He'd made her believe it was true.

Walking past the cast room, Grace could see an elderly woman having a broken wrist plastered. There were people in the minor surgery area, too, with another elderly patient who looked like he was having a skin flap replaced. And then she was walking past the small rooms, their doors open and the interiors empty, but that couldn't stop a memory of the first time she had walked past one of them. When she'd seen those two small faces peering out and she had met Cameron and Max.

It couldn't stop the tight squeeze on her heart as she remembered falling in love with Max when he'd smiled at her and thanked her for fixing his truck and then cuddled up against her. He was more cuddly than his brother but she loved Cameron just as much now.

And their father?

Oh... Grace paused for a moment to grab a cup of water from the cooler before she pushed through the double doors into the coal face of the ER.

It hadn't been love at first sight with Charles.

But it had been love at first *night*.

That was why she'd been so nervous about working with him again. He'd surprised her by calling her that night about the dog-sitting possibility by revealing that he'd been thinking about her.

And he'd made her laugh. Made her drop her guard a little?

She'd realised soon after that that the connection was still there. The way he'd looked at her that day at the park—as if he really wanted to hear her story.

As if he really cared.

Oh, and that *kiss*. In that wreck of a kitchen still redolent with the smells of grilled cheese and freshly baked cookies. Even now, Grace could remember the fear that had stepped in when he'd been about to touch her breast. As though the lumpy scars beneath her clothing had suddenly been flashing like neon signs.

Crumpling the empty polystyrene cup, she dropped it into the bin beside the cooler, catching her bottom lip between her teeth as if she wanted to hide a smile.

They hadn't mattered last night, those scars. She'd barely been aware of them herself…

She was back in the department now and she could see a new patient being wheeled into Resus.

So many patients came and went from that intensive diagnostic and treatment area but some were so much more memorable than others.

Like the first patient she had ever dealt with here. That badly injured cyclist who'd been a casualty of the power cut when the traffic lights had gone out. And the frozen baby that she and Charles had miraculously brought back to life. Yep… Grace would never forget that one.

That time with just the two of them when it had seemed as if time had been somehow rewound and that there was nothing standing between herself and Charles. No social differences that had put them on separate planets all those years ago. No past history of partners who had been loved and lost. No barriers apart from the defensive walls they had both constructed and maybe that had been the moment when Grace had believed there might be a way through those barriers.

She'd been right. And Helena had been right in noticing that there was something different about her today.

The only thing that could have made her even happier would be to feel the vibration against her waistband that would advertise an incoming text message.

But it didn't happen. Case after case took her attention during the next few hours. An asthmatic child who had forgotten his inhaler in the excitement of heading to watch the parade and suffered an attack that meant an urgent trip to the nearest ER. A man who'd had his foot stepped on by a horse. A woman who'd been caught up in the crowd when the first pains of her miscarriage had struck.

Case after case and the time flew by and Grace focused on each and every case as if it was the only thing that mattered. To stop herself checking her phone? It was well past lunchtime when she finally took a break in a deserted staffroom and sat down with a cup of coffee and could no longer ignore the weight and shape of her phone. No way to avoid glancing at it. At a blank screen that had no new messages or missed calls flagged.

Anxiety crept in as she stared at that blank screen. Was Charles sick or injured or had something happened to one of the twins? She could forgive this silence if that was the case but it would have to be something major like that because to treat her like this again when he knew how it would make her feel was... well, it was unforgiveable. All he'd had to do was send a simple message. A stupid smiley face would have been enough. Surely he would understand that every minute of continuing silence would feel like hours? That hours would actually start to feel like days?

But if something major like that had happened, she would have heard about it. Like she'd heard about Miranda being caught up in that tunnel collapse. A thread of anger took over from anxiety. How could she have allowed herself to get into a position where everything she had worked so hard for was under threat? She had come to New York to start a new life. To move on from so much loss. The loss of her marriage. The loss of the family she'd dreamed of having. The loss of feeling desirable, even.

Charles had given her a glimpse of a future that could have filled all those empty places in her soul.

This silence felt like a warning shot that it was no more than an illusion.

That the extraordinary happiness she had brought to work with her was no more than a puff of breath on an icy morning. The kind she had been making as she'd walked to Manhattan Mercy this morning in a haze of happiness after last night.

Last night?

It was beginning to feel like a lifetime ago. A lifetime in which this scenario had already played out to a miserable ending.

Anxiety and anger both gave way to doubt.

Had she really thought that history couldn't repeat itself? This was certainly beginning to feel like a re-run.

Maybe it had only been in her imagination that her scars didn't matter.

Maybe having a woman in his bed had opened old wounds for Charles and he was realising how much he missed Nina and that no one could ever take her place.

Maybe it had been too much, too soon and everything had been ruined.

For a moment, Grace considered sending another message. Just something casual, like asking whether they'd been to the parade this morning or saying that she hoped they were all having a good day.

But this new doubt was strong enough to make her hesitate and, in that moment of hesitation, she knew she couldn't do it.

Her confidence was starting to ebb away just as quickly as that happiness.

CHAPTER NINE

ANOTHER HOUR WENT past and then another...
and still nothing.

Nothing...

No call. No text. No serendipitous meeting
as their paths crossed in the ER, which was
such a normal thing to happen that its absence
was starting to feel deliberate.

Grace knew Charles had finally come to
work this afternoon because the door to his
office was open and she'd seen his leather laptop bag on his desk when she'd gone past a
while back. She'd heard someone say he was in
a meeting, which wasn't unusual for the chief
of emergency services, but surely there weren't
administrative issues that would take hours
and hours to discuss? Maybe it hadn't actually been that long but it was certainly beginning to feel like it.

She thought she saw him heading for the

unit desk when she slipped through a curtain, intending to chase up the first test results on one of her patients.

Her heart skipped a beat and started racing.

She'd know, wouldn't she? In that first instant of eye contact, she'd know exactly what was going on. She'd know whether it had been a huge mistake to get this close to Charles Davenport again. To be so completely in love and have so many shiny hopes for a new future that were floating around her like fragile, newly blown bubbles.

She'd know whether she was going to find herself right back at Square One in rebuilding her life.

Almost in the same instant, however, and even though she couldn't see his face properly, she knew it wasn't Charles, it was his twin, Elijah. And she knew this because the air she was sucking into her lungs felt completely normal. There was none of that indefinable extra energy that permeated the atmosphere when she was in the same space as Charles. The energy that made those bubbles shine with iridescent colours and change their shape as if they were dancing in response to the sizzle of hope.

'Dr Forbes?'

The tone in her migraine patient's voice made her swing back, letting the curtain fall into place behind her.

'I'm going to be sick…'

Grace grabbed a vomit container but she was too late. A nurse responded swiftly to her call for assistance and her gaze was sympathetic.

'I'll clean up in here,' she said. 'You'd better go and find some clean scrubs.' Pulling on gloves, she added a murmur that their patient couldn't overhear. 'It's been one of *those* days, hasn't it?'

Helena was in the linen supply room.

'Oh, no…' She wrinkled her nose. 'You poor thing…'

'Do we have any plastic bags in here? For super-soiled laundry?'

'Over there. Want me to guard the door for a minute so you can strip that lot off?'

'Please. I'm starting to feel a bit queasy myself.'

'Do you need a shower?'

'No. It's just on my scrubs.' Grace unhooked her stethoscope and then unclipped her phone and pager from her waistband. She put them onto a stainless-steel trolley and then peeled off her tunic. 'What are you doing in here, anyway?'

'We were low on blankets in the warmer and everyone was busy. I'm due for a break.' Helena was leaning against the closed door, blocking the small window. 'Past due to go home, in fact. We both are.' Her smile was rueful. 'How come we were among the ones to offer to stay on?'

'We were short-staffed and overloaded. It was lucky Sarah Grayson could stay on as well.'

'I know. Well, I've hardly seen you since this morning. You okay?' She wrinkled her nose. 'Sorry—silly question. Crazy day, huh?'

'Mmm.' Grace was folding the tunic carefully so she could put it into the bag without touching the worst stains. 'I certainly wouldn't want another one like this in a hurry.'

Not that staying on past her rostered hours had bothered her, mind you. Or the patient load. She loved a professional challenge. It was the personal challenge she was in the middle of that was a lot less welcome.

'What are you doing after work? There's a group going out for Thanksgiving dinner at a local restaurant that sounds like it might be fun. I know you'd be more than welcome.'

But, again, Grace shook her head. 'I can't abandon my dog after being at work so much longer than expected. And I need to Skype my dad. I haven't spoken to him for a while and it's Thanksgiving. Family time.'

'Ah…' Helena's gaze was mischievous. 'And there was me thinking you might be going to some glitzy Davenport occasion.'

Pulling on her clean scrub trousers, Grace let the elastic waist band go with more force than necessary. 'What?'

'You and Charles…?' Helena was smiling now. 'Is *that* why you were looking so happy first thing this morning? Everybody's wondering…'

A heavy knot formed in Grace's gut. People were gossiping about her? And Charles? Had he said something to someone else when he hadn't bothered talking to her? Or had someone seen something or said something to remind Charles that he would never be able to replace his beloved wife? Maybe *that* was why he was ignoring her.

'I have no idea what you're talking about,' she said. 'We're just friends.'

'That's what he said, too.'

'What?' Grace fought the shock wave that made it difficult to move. *'When?'*

'There was someone here earlier this afternoon. A journalist pretending to be a patient and she was asking for you. You'd taken a patient off for an MRI, I think. Or maybe you were finally having a late lunch. Anyway... Charles told her she was wasting her time. That you were nothing more than a colleague and friend. And never would be.'

Was it simply the waft of soiled laundry that was making Grace feel a little faint? She secured the top of the plastic bag and shoved it into the contaminated linen sack.

So she didn't need to make eye contact with Charles to know that the truth was every bit as gut wrenching as she had suspected it would be.

'I don't understand,' she murmured. 'Why was he even saying anything?'

'It's because of the gossip column. That photo. Any Davenport news is going to be jumped on around here. They're like New York royalty.'

'What gossip column? What *photo*?'

'You don't know?' Helena's eyes widened. 'Look. I can show you on my phone. I have to admit, you do look like a really happy little family...'

* * *

Focus, Charles reminded himself. Shut out anything irrelevant that's only going to make everything worse.

He had responsibilities that took priority over any personal discomfort.

His boys came first. He'd been a little later for work this afternoon, after getting home from the parade, because he'd needed to brief Maria about the renewed media interest in his life and warn her not to say anything about his private life if she was approached by a journalist. He was going to keep the boys away from nursery school for a day or two, as well, for the same reason.

He'd assumed that he'd see Grace at work and be able to have a quiet word and warn her that she might be faced with some unwelcome attention but she hadn't been in the department when he'd arrived. Instead, he'd been confronted with the reality that interest in the Davenport family's private lives was never going to vanish. How had someone found out that Grace worked here? Had it helped to deal so brusquely with that journalist who had been masquerading as a patient or had he protested too much?

At least Grace hadn't been there to hear him

dismissing her as someone who would never be anything more significant than a friend but the echo of his own words was haunting him now.

It wasn't true. He might have no idea how to handle these unexpected emotions that were undermining everything in his personal life that he'd believed would never change but the thing he could be certain of was that his own feelings were irrelevant right now.

He was in a meeting, for heaven's sake, where his push for additional resources in his department was dependent on being able to defend the statistics of patient outcomes and being able to explain anomalies in terms of scientific reasoning that was balanced by morality and the mission statements of Manhattan Mercy's emergency room.

He had to focus.

One meeting merged into the next until it was late in the day and he was still caught up in a boardroom. The detailed report of how his department and others had coped in the power cut last month was up for discussion with the purpose of making sure that they would be better prepared if it should ever happen again.

It was hard to focus in this meeting as well. The day of the power cut had been the day that

Grace Forbes had walked back into his life in more than a professional sense. It seemed like fate had been determined to bring her close as quickly as possible. How else could he explain the series of events that had led her to meet his sons and remind him of how lucky he actually was? That had been when his barriers had been weakened, he realised. When that curiosity about Grace had put her into a different space than any other woman could have reached.

The kind of determination to focus that was needed here was reminiscent of one of the most difficult times of his life—when he'd had to try and pass his final exams in medicine while the fallout of the Davenport scandal had been exploding around him. How hard that had been had been eclipsed by the tragedy of Nina's death, of course, but he'd somehow coped then as well.

And he could cope now.

'We can't base future plans on the normal throughput of the department,' he reminded the people gathered in this boardroom. 'What we have to factor in is that this kind of widespread disruption causes a huge spike in admissions due to the accidents directly caused by it. Fortunately, it's a rare event so we can't resource the department to be ready at all times. What we can do is have a management plan in place that will put us in the best position to deal with whatever disaster we find on our doorstep. And haven't there been predictions already for severe snow storms in December? If it's correct, that could also impact our power supply and patient numbers.'

By the time his meeting finished, a new shift was staffing the department and Grace was nowhere to be seen.

He could knock on her door when he got home, Charles decided, but a glance at his watch told him that he'd have to be quick. He was due to take the boys to their grandparents' house for Thanksgiving dinner tonight and he was already running late.

Was she even at home? He'd heard about the staff dinner at a restaurant being planned and, when there was no response to his knock other than a warning bark from Houston, he hoped that was exactly where she was.

Out having fun.

More fun than he was likely to have tonight, with his mother still stressed about renewed media interest in the family and the necessity of trying to keep two three-year-old boys behaving themselves at a very formal dining table.

Maria had got the boys dressed and said she didn't mind waiting while he got changed himself. A quick shower was needed and then Charles found his dinner jacket and bow tie. The formality was a family tradition, like getting the annual Davenport photograph that would be made available to the media to remind them that this family was still together. Still strong enough to survive anything.

Charles rummaged in the top drawer of his dresser, to find the box that contained his silver cufflinks. He didn't know how many of the family members would be there tonight but hopefully the table would be full. Elijah would definitely be there. And Zac, who was about to start his new job at Manhattan Mercy.

His fingers closed around a velvet box and he opened it, only to have his breath catch in his throat.

This wasn't the box that contained his cufflinks. It was the box that contained the Davenport ring. The astonishing pink diamond that Nina had accepted when she had accepted his proposal of marriage. A symbol of the continuation of the Davenport name. A symbol of their position in New York society, even, given the value and rarity of this famous stone.

As the oldest son, it had been given to Charles for his wife-to-be and there was only one person in the world who could have worn it.

Nina.

Shadows of old grief enclosed Charles as he stared at the ring. He could never give it to anyone else.

It wouldn't even suit Grace…

Oh, help…where had *that* come from?

Memories of how he'd felt waking up this morning came back to him in a rush. That excitement. The pleasure.

The…longing…

And right now, those feelings were at war with remnants of grief. With the weight of all the responsibilities he had been trying so hard to focus on.

The battle was leaving him even more confused.

Drained, even.

He left the ring in its opened box on top of the dresser as he found and inserted his cufflinks and then slipped on his silk-lined jacket.

He closed the box on the ring then, and was

about to put it back where he'd found it but his hand stopped in mid-air.

He had no right to keep this ring shut away in a drawer when he had no intention of ever using it again himself. It could be hidden for decades if he waited to hand it on to his first-born, Cameron.

He should give it to the next Davenport in line. Elijah.

Charles let his breath out in a sigh. He knew perfectly well how his twin felt about marriage. With his bitterness about the marriage of their parents and scepticism about its value in general, he wouldn't want anything to do with the Davenport ring.

He couldn't give it to Penelope, because it was traditional for it to go to a son who would be carrying on the family name. Miranda was out of the question, even if she hadn't been another female, because of the distress that could cause to his mother, given her reluctance to absorb his half-sister into the family.

Zac. Was that his answer? The youngest Davenport male in his own generation. Okay, Zac had always had a tendency to rebel against Davenport traditions but he was making an effort now, wasn't he? Coming back into the fold. Trying to rebuild bridges? Was it possible that could even extend to taking an interest in Dr Ella Lockwood, the daughter of family friends and the woman who everyone had once expected Zac to marry? Though he'd noticed Ella hadn't seemed too pleased to learn that Zac was joining the team, so maybe not. But whatever happened, he hoped his youngest brother would find the happiness he deserved.

Yes. Charles slipped the ring box into his pocket. Even if Zac wasn't ready to accept it yet, he would know that it would be waiting for him.

He'd have a word with Elijah, first, of course. And then Zac. Maybe with his parents as well. If he could handle it all diplomatically, it could actually be a focus for this evening that would bring them all a little closer together and distract them from directing any attention on his own life. It would also be a symbol that he was moving on from his past, too. For himself as much as his family.

Yes. This felt like the next step in dealing with this unexpected intrusion into their lives. And maybe it would help settle the confusing boundaries between his responsibilities and his desires. Between the determination to protect everyone he had cared about in his life so far and the longing to just be somewhere alone with the new person in his life that he also wanted to protect?

Grace heard the knock on her door.

But what could she do? Her father had just answered her Skype call and he was so delighted to see her.

If there'd been a second knock, she might have excused herself for a moment but, after a single bark, Houston came and settled himself with his head on her feet. There was obviously no one on the other side of the door now. Maybe it had been someone else who lived in this apartment block. After all, Charles had had an entire day in which he could have called or texted her. Or he could have found her at work this afternoon because she'd certainly hung around long enough.

And he hadn't.

History was clearly repeating itself.

She had offered him everything she had to give and he had accepted it and then simply walked away without a backward glance.

'Sorry—what was that, Dad?'

'Just saying we hit the national high again

today. Blue skies and sunshine here in Florida. How's it looking in the big smoke?'

'Grey. And freezing. They're predicting snow tomorrow. It could be heavy.'

Her father laughed. 'We have hospitals in this neck of the woods, you know. You don't have to suffer!'

'Maybe I'll see what's being advertised.'

The comment was light-hearted but, as they chatted about other things, the thought stayed in the back of her mind.

She could walk away from New York, couldn't she? She didn't *have* to stay here and feel...rejected...

Grace had to swallow a sudden lump in her throat. 'I feel a long way away at the moment. I miss you, Dad.'

'Miss you, too, honey.' Her father's smile wobbled a bit. 'So tell me, what are you doing for Thanksgiving dinner? Have you got yourself some turkey?'

'No. Work's been really busy and, anyway, it seemed a bit silly buying a turkey for one person.'

'I'll bet that dog you're living with could have helped you out there.'

Grace laughed but her brain was racing down another track. It couldn't have been

Charles knocking at her door because wasn't he going to some big Davenport family dinner tonight? A dinner that he had suggested she could also go to but then he'd made a face as if the idea was distasteful.

Why? Did he not enjoy the family gathering himself or was it more the idea that she would hate it because she wouldn't fit in?

Of course she wouldn't. As Helena had reminded her so recently, the Davenports were New York royalty and she wasn't even American by birth. She was a foreigner. A divorced foreigner. A divorced foreigner with a scarred body who wasn't even capable of becoming a mother.

Oh, help… Going down this track any further when she had a night alone stretching out in front of her was a very bad idea.

'Have you got some wine to go with your turkey, Dad?'

'Of course. A very nice Australian chardonnay.'

'Well…I've got something in the fridge. Prosecco, I think. Why don't we both have a glass together and we can tap the screen and say cheers.' It was hard to summon up a cheerful smile but Grace gave it her best shot.

She could deal with this.

She had, in fact, just had a very good idea of exactly how she could deal with it. When she had finished this call with her dad, and had had a glass or two of wine, she was going to do something very proactive.

It was ironic that it had been Charles who'd pointed out how far she had come from being someone vulnerable enough to be easily crushed. How strong she was now.

Ironic because she was going to write her resignation letter from Manhattan Mercy. And, tomorrow, as soon as she started her shift, it would be Charles Davenport's desk that she would put that letter on.

CHAPTER TEN

'THANKS EVER SO much for coming home, Dr Davenport.'

'It's no problem, Maria. You need to get to this appointment for the final check on that back of yours. I hope you won't need the brace any more after this.'

'I shouldn't be more than a couple of hours. I'll text you if there's any hold-up.'

'Don't worry about it. I've got more than enough work that I can do from home.'

His nanny nodded, wrapping a thick scarf around her neck. 'The boys are happy. They're busy drawing pictures at the moment.'

A glance into the living area showed a coffee table covered with sheets of paper and scattered crayons. Two tousled heads were bent as the twins focused on their masterpieces. Charles stayed where he was for a moment, pulling his phone from his pocket and hitting a rapid-dial key.

'Emergency Room.'

Charles recognised the voice of one of the staff members who managed the phone system and incoming radio calls.

'Hi, Sharon. Charles Davenport here. I'm working from home for a few hours.'

'Yes, we're aware of that, Dr Davenport. Did you want to speak to the other Dr Davenport?'

'No. I actually wanted to speak to Dr Forbes. Is she available at the moment?'

'Hang on, I'll check.'

Charles could hear the busy sounds of the department through the line but it sounded a little calmer than it had been earlier today. When he'd gone to his office to collect his briefcase after the latest meeting, there'd been security personnel and police officers there but Elijah had assured him that everything was under control and he was free to take the time he needed away.

Right now, the voices close by were probably doctors checking lab results or X-rays on the computers. Would one of them be Grace, by any chance?

He hadn't seen her when he'd been in at work earlier and this was getting ridiculous.

It was well into the second day after their night together and they hadn't even spoken. His intention to protect everyone he cared about by ignoring the potential for public scrutiny on his private life had been so strong, it was only now that it was beginning to feel like something was very wrong.

No. Make that more than 'feel'. He knew that he was in trouble.

He'd met the Australian dog walker, Kylie, in the foyer on his way in, minutes ago. The one that looked after Houston when Grace was at work.

She'd introduced herself. Because, she explained, she might be in residence for a while—if Grace left before Houston's owners were due to return.

But Stefan and Jerome had been planning to come back in less than a couple of weeks as far as Charles was aware.

Why would Grace be thinking of leaving before then?

It had only been just over a day since he'd seen her. How could something that huge have changed so much in such a short space of time?

He needed to speak to her. To apologise for not having spoken to her yesterday. At the very least, he had to arrange a time when they could talk. To find out what was going on.

To repair any damage he had the horrible feeling he might be responsible for? He'd tried so hard to do things perfectly this time—to think through each step logically so that he could avoid making a mistake.

But he'd missed something. Something that was seeming increasingly important.

Sharon was back on the line.

'Sorry, Dr Davenport. Dr Forbes is in CT at the moment. We had a head injury patient earlier who was extremely combative. We had to call Security in to help restrain him while he got sedated and intubated.'

'Yes, I saw them there when I was leaving.'

'He was Dr Forbes's patient. She's gone with him to CT and may have to stay with him if he needs to go to Theatre so I have no idea how long she'll be. Do you want me to page her to call you back when she can?'

'Daddy... *Daddy*...' Cameron was tugging on his arm, a sheet of paper in his other hand. 'Look at *this*.'

'No, thanks, Sharon. She's busy enough, by the sound of things. I'll catch up with her later.'

He ended the call. Was he kidding himself? He'd been trying to 'catch up' with her from the moment he'd arrived at work yesterday and it hadn't happened. And suddenly he felt like he was chasing something that was rapidly disappearing into the distance.

'Daddy? What's the matter?'

The concern in Max's voice snapped Charles back to where he was. He crouched down as Max joined his brother.

'Nothing's the matter, buddy.'

'But you look sad.'

'No-o-o…' Charles ruffled the heads of both his boys. 'How could I be sad when I get to spend some extra time with you guys? Hey… did you really draw that picture all by yourself?' He reached out for the paper to admire the artwork more closely but, to his surprise, Max shook his head and stepped back.

'It's for Gace,' he said solemnly.

'So's mine,' Cameron said. 'But you can look.'

The colourful scribbles were getting more recognisable these days. A stick figure person with a huge, crooked smile. And another one with too many legs.

'It's Gace. And Horse.'

'Aww…she'll love them. You know what?'

'What?'

'I'll bet she puts them in a frame and puts them on her wall.'

The boys beamed at him but then Max's smile wobbled.

'And then she'll come back?'

Why hadn't it occurred to him how much the twins were already missing Grace? How much they loved her as well as Horse. He hadn't factored that in when he'd chosen to distance himself enough to keep his family temporarily out of the spotlight, had he? When he'd left her text unanswered and had told that journalist that they were nothing more than friends.

And never would be.

How many people had overheard that comment? Passed it on, even?

Could *that* have been enough to persuade Grace that she didn't want to be in New York any more?

The sinking sensation that had begun with that chance meeting with Kylie gained momentum and crashed into the pit of Charles's stomach but he smiled reassuringly and nodded.

It was tantamount to a promise, that smile and nod. A promise that Grace would be back. Now he just had to find a way to make sure he didn't let his boys down.

'You guys hungry? Want some cookies and milk? And *Curious George* on TV?'

'*Yes!*'

At least three-year-old boys were easily distracted.

Or maybe not.

'*Spider* cookies,' Cameron shouted. 'They're the bestest.'

'I think we've run out of spider cookies,' he apologised.

'That's okay, Daddy.' Max patted his arm. 'I'll tell Gace and we'll help her make some more.'

He had to sit down with the boys and supervise the milk drinking but Charles wasn't taking any notice of the monkey's antics on the screen that were sending the twins into fits of giggles.

His mind was somewhere else entirely, carried away by the echo of his son's words. The tone of his voice.

That confidence that everything would be put to rights when he'd had the chance to explain what was wrong to Grace.

It hadn't even occurred to either of his boys to suggest that *he* make them some more home-made cookies. It might be only a superficial example but it symbolised all those things a mother could do that perhaps he couldn't even recognise as being missing from their lives.

And that longing in Max's voice.

And then she'll come back?

It touched something very deep inside Charles. Opened the door he'd shut in his head and heart that was a space that was filled with the same longing. Not just for a woman in his life or for sex. That need was there, of course, but this longing—it was for Grace.

He had to do a whole lot more than simply apologise for leaving her text unanswered when he spoke to her. He had to make her understand how important she'd become to his boys. How much they loved her.

And…and he had to tell her that he felt the same way.

That *he* loved her.

That the idea of life without her had become something unthinkable.

There was a painful lump in his throat that he tried to clear away but that only made Max look up at him with those big, blue eyes that could often see so much more than you'd expect a small boy to see.

'You happy, Daddy?'

'Sure am, buddy.' Man, it was hard work

to sound as though he meant it. 'You finished with that milk?'

He took the empty cups back to the kitchen. He glanced at his phone lying on the table beside his laptop on his return.

Was it worth trying to find out if Grace was available?

There was a sense of urgency about this now. What if she really was planning to leave? What if she was actually planning to leave New York? Surely she wouldn't do that without telling him?

But why would she?

He hadn't spoken to her since they'd spent the night together. He hadn't even answered her text message.

Okay, stuff had happened and events had conspired to prevent him seeing her the way he'd assumed he'd be able to, but the truth was there was no excuse for what the combination of things had produced. Without any intention of doing so, he had allowed history to repeat itself. He'd made love to Grace and then seemingly ignored her. Pushed her out of his life because something else had seemed more important.

So why wouldn't she just walk away?

He'd thought he was protecting her by not

giving any journalists a reason to pry into her life when there were things that he knew she would prefer to keep very private.

Those same things that had made her so vulnerable to allowing herself to get close to another man.

Why had he assumed that she needed his protection anyway? As he'd reminded her himself, she was a strong, courageous woman and she had dealt with far worse things in her life than the threat of having her privacy invaded.

She had been courageous enough to take the risk of letting *him* that close.

And somehow—albeit unintentionally—he'd repeated the same mistake he'd made the first time.

He'd made everything worse.

He hadn't even been protecting his boys in one sense, either. He'd created the risk of them losing someone they loved. Someone they needed in their lives.

Charles rubbed the back of his neck, lifting his gaze as he tried to fight his way through this mess in his head. The view from the massive windows caught his attention for a blessed moment of distraction. It was beginning to snow heavily. Huge, fat flakes were drifting down, misting the view of the Manhattan sky-line and Central Park.

Charles loved snow. He'd never quite lost that childish excitement of seeing it fall or waking up to find his world transformed by the soft, white blanket of a thick covering. But there wasn't even a spark of that excitement right now. All he could feel was that lump-inducing longing. A bone-deep need to be close to Grace.

He'd never thought he'd ever feel like this again. He'd never wanted to after Nina had died because the grief had been crippling and he never wanted to face another loss like that. He didn't want his boys to have to face that kind of loss, either.

But it had happened. He had fallen in love. Maybe it had always been there, in an enforced hibernation after that first night they'd been together, thanks to the life events that had happened afterwards.

And here he was, possibly facing the loss of this love and, in a way, it would be worse than losing Nina because Grace would still be alive. If she wasn't actually planning on leaving Manhattan Mercy, and was only thinking of finding a new place to live, he'd see her at work and see that smile and hear her voice and know that being together could have been possible if he'd done things differently.

There had to be some way he could fix this.

If Grace had feelings for him that were anything like as powerful as the ones he had finally recognised, surely there was a way to put things right.

But how?

A phone call couldn't do it.

Even a conversation might not be enough.

Charles took a deep inward breath and then let it out very slowly as he watched the flakes continuing to fall. This was no passing shower. This snow would settle. Maybe not for long. It would probably be slush by the morning if the temperature lifted but for the next few hours at least it would look like a different world out there.

A world that Grace had been so eager to see.

An echo of her voice whispered in his mind.

'It's always been my dream for Christmas. A sleigh ride in a snowy park. At night, when there's sparkly lights everywhere and there are bells on the horses and you have to be all wrapped up in soft blankets.'

He could have given her that. But how likely was it to be possible now? Christmas was weeks away and maybe she wouldn't even be here.

He needed a small miracle.

And as he stood there, watching the snow fall, Charles became aware of the spark that had been missing. Excitement about the snow?

Maybe.

Or maybe it was just hope.

The letter was still in her pocket.

Grace could feel it crinkle as she sat down on the chair beside her elderly patient's bed.

She could have gone in and put it on Charles Davenport's desk first thing this morning but she hadn't.

Because he'd been in the office. Sitting at his desk, his head bent, clearly focused on the paperwork in front of him. And it had been just too hard to know what it would be like to meet his eyes. To explain what was in the sealed envelope in her hands. To have the conversation that might have suggested they were both adults and surely they could continue working together. To be friends, even?

Nope. She didn't think she could do that. Okay, maybe it was cowardly to leave a letter and run away. She was going to have to work out her notice and that meant that they would be working in the same space for the next couple of weeks but she would cope with that the same way she was going to cope today. By immersing herself in her work to the exclusion of absolutely everything else.

And fate seemed set to help her do exactly that, by providing an endless stream of patients that needed her complete focus.

Like the guy this morning. A victim of assault but it was highly likely he'd started the fight himself. The huge and very aggressive man had presented a danger to all staff involved with his care, despite the presence of the police escort who'd brought him in. Security had had to be called and it had been a real challenge to sedate this patient and get him on a ventilator. Due to his size, the drugs needed to keep him sedated were at a high level and Grace had needed to monitor their effects very closely. Knowing what could happen if his levels dropped meant that she'd had to stay with him while he went to CT and then to Theatre so the case had taken up a good part of her morning.

Charles was nowhere to be seen when she was back in the ER but, even if he had been there, she could have kept herself almost invisible behind the curtains of various cubicles or the resuscitation areas. Patient after patient came under her care. A man with a broken finger who'd needed a nerve block before it could be realigned and splinted. A stroke victim. Two heart attacks. A woman who'd slipped on the snow that was apparently starting to fall outside and had a compound tib and fib fracture and no circulation in her foot.

And now she was in a side room with a very elderly woman called Mary who had been brought in a couple of hours ago in severe respiratory distress from an advanced case of pneumonia. Mary was eighty-six years old and had adamantly refused to have any treatment other than something to make her more comfortable.

'It's my time,' she'd told Grace quietly. 'I don't want to fight any more.'

Grace had called up her patient's notes. Mary had had a double mastectomy for breast cancer more than thirty years ago and only a few weeks back she had been diagnosed with ovarian cancer. She had refused treatment then as well. While it was difficult, as a doctor, to stand by and not provide treatment that could help, like antibiotics, it was Mary's right to make this decision and her reasoning was understandable. Very much of sound mind, she had smiled very sweetly at Grace and squeezed her hand.

'You're a darling to be so concerned but please don't worry. I'm not afraid.'

'Do you have any family we can call? Or close friends?'

'There was only ever my Billy. And he's waiting for me. He's been waiting a long time now…'

Helena had been concerned that Grace was caring for this patient.

'I can take her,' she said. 'I know how hard this must be for you. Your mum died of ovarian cancer, didn't she?'

Grace nodded, swallowing past the constriction in her throat. 'I sat with her at the end, too. Right now it feels like it was yesterday.'

'Which is why you should step back, maybe. We'll make her as comfortable as possible in one of the private rooms out the back. It could take a while, you know. I'll find a nurse to sit with her so she won't be alone.'

'She knows me now. And I don't care how long it takes, as long as you can cope without me in here?'

'Of course. But—'

'It's because of my mum that I'm the right person to do this,' Grace said softly. 'Because of how real it feels for me. I want to do this for Mary. I want her to know that she's with someone who really cares.'

So, here they were. In one of the rooms she had noticed on her very first day here when she had wondered what they might be used for. It might even be the room next door to the one that she had stayed in with the twins and fixed Max's fire truck but this one had a bed with a comfortable air mattress. It was warm and softly lit. There was an oxygen port that was providing a little comfort to ease how difficult it was for Mary to breathe and there was a trolley that contained the drugs Grace might need to keep her from any undue distress. The morphine had taken away her pain and made her drowsy but they had talked off and on for the last hour and Grace knew that her husband Billy had died suddenly ten years ago.

'I'm so glad he didn't know about this new cancer,' Mary whispered. 'He would have been so upset. He was so good to me the first time...'

She knew that they had met seventy years ago at a summer event in Central Park.

'People say that there's no such thing as true love at first sight. But we knew different, Billy and me...'

She knew that they'd never had children.

'We never got blessed like that. It wasn't so hard...we had each other and that was enough...'

In the last half an hour Mary had stopped talking and her breathing had become shallow and rapid. Grace knew that she was still aware of her surroundings, however, because every so often she would feel a gentle squeeze from the hand her own fingers were curled around.

And finally that laboured breathing hitched and then stopped and Mary slipped away so quietly and peacefully that Grace simply sat there, still holding her hand, for the longest time.

It didn't matter now that she had tears rolling down her cheeks. She wasn't sad, exactly. Mary had believed that she was about to be reunited with her love and she had welcomed the release from any more suffering. She hadn't died alone, either. She had been grateful for Grace's company. For a hand to hold.

And she'd been lucky, hadn't she?

She had known true love. Had loved and been loved in equal measure.

Or maybe she *was* sad.

Not for Mary, but for herself.

Grace had come so close to finding that sort

of love for herself—or she'd thought she had. But now, it seemed as far away as ever. As if she was standing on the other side of a plate-glass window, looking in at a scene that she couldn't be a part of.

A perfect scene.

A Christmas one, perhaps. With pretty lights on a tree and parcels tied up with bows underneath. A fire in a grate beneath a mantelpiece that had colourful stockings hanging from it. There were people in that scene, too. A tall man with dark hair and piercing blue eyes. Two little mop-topped, happy boys. And a big, curly, adorable dog.

It took a while to get those overwhelming emotions under control but the company of this brave old woman who had unexpectedly appeared in her life helped, so by the time Grace alerted others of Mary's death, nobody would have guessed how much it had affected her. They probably just thought she looked very tired and who wouldn't, after such a long day?

It took a while after that to do what was necessary after a death of a patient and it was past time for Grace's shift to finish by the time she bundled herself up in her warm coat and scarf and gloves, ready for her walk home.

She walked out of the ER via the ambulance

bay and found that it had been snowing far more than she'd been told about. A soft blanket of whiteness had cloaked everything and the world had that muted sound that came with snow when even the traffic was almost silent. And it was cold. Despite her gloves, Grace could feel her fingers tingling so she shoved her hands in her pockets and that was when she felt the crinkle of that envelope again.

Thanks to her time with Mary, she had completely forgotten to put it on Charles's desk.

Perhaps that was a good thing?

Running away from something because it was difficult wasn't the kind of person she was now.

Charles had told her how courageous she was. He had made her believe it and that belief had been enough to push her into risking her heart again.

And that had to be a good thing, too.

Even if it didn't feel like it right now.

She had almost reached the street now where the lamps were casting a circle of light amidst a swirl of snowflakes but she turned back, hesitating.

She hadn't even looked in the direction of Charles's office when she'd left. Maybe he was still there?

Maybe the kind of person she was now would actually go back and talk about this. Take the risk of making herself even more vulnerable?

And that was when she heard it.

Someone calling her name.

No. It was a jingle of bells. She had just imagined hearing her name.

She turned back to the road and any need to make a decision on what direction she was about to take evaporated.

There was a sleigh just outside the ambulance entrance to Manhattan Mercy.

A bright red sleigh, with swirling gold patterns on its sides and a canopy that was rimmed with fairy lights. A single white horse was in front, its red harness covered with small bells and, on its head—instead of the usual feathery plume—it had a set of reindeer antlers.

A driver sat in the front, a dark shape in a heavy black coat and scarf and top hat. But, in the back, there was someone else.

Charles...

'Grace...?'

Her legs were taking her forward without any instruction from her brain.

She was too stunned to be thinking of anything, in fact. Other than that Charles was here.

In a *sleigh*?

Maybe she'd got that image behind the plate-glass window a little wrong earlier.

Maybe *this* was the magic place she hadn't been able to reach.

Just Charles. In a sleigh. In the snow.

And he was holding out his hand now, to invite her to join him under the canopy at the back. Waiting to help her reach that place.

Grace was still too stunned to be aware of any coherent thoughts but her body seemed to know what to do and she found herself reaching up to take that hand.

She had been on the point of summoning the courage to go and find Charles even if it meant stepping into the most vulnerable space she could imagine.

Here she was, literally stepping into that space.

And it hadn't taken as much courage as she'd expected.

Because it felt…right…

Because it was Charles who was reaching out to her and there was no way on earth she could have turned away.

CHAPTER ELEVEN

HEART-WRENCHING...

That look on Grace's face when she'd seen him waiting for her in the sleigh.

He'd expected her to be surprised, of course. The sleigh might not be genuine but the sides had been cleverly designed to cover most of the wheels so it not only looked the part but was a pretty unusual sight on a New York street. Along with the bells and fairy lights and the reindeer antlers on the horse, he had already been a target for every phone or camera that people had been able to produce.

For once, he didn't mind the attention. Bundled up in his thick coat and scarf, with a hat pulled well down over his head, Charles Davenport was unrecognisable but the worry about publicity was a million miles from his mind, anyway. The sight of this spectacle—that had taken him most of the day to organise—didn't just make people want to capture the image. It was delighting them, making them point and wave. To smile and laugh.

But Grace hadn't smiled when she saw him. She'd looked shocked.

Scared, almost?

So, so vulnerable that Charles knew in that instant just how much damage his silence had caused.

And how vital it was to fix it.

The sheer relief when Grace had accepted his hand to climb up into the carriage had been so overwhelming that perhaps he couldn't blame the biting cold for making his eyes water. Or for making it too hard to say anything just yet. How much courage had it taken for her to accept his hand?

He loved her for that courage. And for everything else he knew to be true about her.

And nothing needed to be said just yet. For now, it was too important to make sure that Grace was going to be warm enough. To pull one faux fur blanket after another from the pile at his feet, to wrap them both in a soft cocoon. A single cocoon, so that as soon as he was satisfied there was no danger of hypothermia, he could wrap his arms around Grace beneath these blankets and simply hold her close.

Extra protection from the cold?

No. This was about protecting what he knew was the most important thing in his life at this moment. Grace. So important in his boys' lives as well. The only thing he wasn't sure of yet was how important it might be in her life.

The steady, rocking motion of the carriage was like a slow heartbeat that made him acutely aware of every curve in the body of the woman he was holding and, as the driver finished negotiating traffic and turned into the lamplit, almost deserted paths of Central Park, he could feel the tension in Grace's body begin to lessen. It was under the halo of one of those antique streetlamps that Grace finally raised her head to meet his gaze and he could see that the shock had worn off.

There was something else in her gaze now. Hope?

That wouldn't be there, would it? Unless this was just as important to her as it was to him?

Again, the rush of emotion made it impossible to find any words.

Instead, Charles bent his head and touched Grace's lips gently with his own. Her lips parted beneath his and he felt the astonishing warmth of her mouth. Of her breath.

A breath of life...

Maybe he still didn't need to say anything yet. Or maybe he could say it another way...

For the longest time, Grace's brain had been stunned into immobility. She was aware of what was around her but couldn't begin to understand what any of it meant.

Her senses were oddly heightened. The softness of the furry blankets felt like she was being wrapped inside a cloud. The motion of the carriage was like being rocked in someone's arms. And then she *was* in someone's arms. Charles's. Grace didn't want to think about what this meant. She just wanted to feel it. This sense of being in the one place in the world she most wanted to be. This feeling of being protected.

Precious...

Finally, she had to raise her head. To check whether this was real. Had she slipped in the snow and knocked herself out cold, perhaps? Was this dream-come-to-life no more than an elaborate creation of her subconscious?

If it was, it couldn't have conjured up a more compelling expression in the eyes of the man she loved.

It was a gaze that told her she was the only thing in the world that mattered right now.

That she was loved…

And then his lips touched her own and Grace could feel how cold they were, which only intensified the heat that was coming from inside his body. From his breath. From the touch of his tongue.

She wasn't unconscious.

Grace had never felt more alive in her life.

It was the longest, most tender kiss she had ever experienced. A whole conversation in itself.

An apology from Charles, definitely. A declaration of love, even.

And on her part? A statement that the agony of his silence and distance since they'd last been together didn't matter, perhaps. That she forgave him. That nothing mattered other than being together, like this.

They had to come up for air eventually, however, and the magic of the kiss retreated.

Actions might speak a whole lot louder than words, but words were important, too.

Charles was the first to use some.

'I'm so sorry,' he said. 'It's been crazy…but when Kylie told me this morning that you were thinking of leaving, I got enough of a shock to realise just how much I'd messed this up.'

'You didn't even answer my text message,'

Grace whispered, her voice cracking. 'The morning after we'd...we'd...'

'I know. I'm sorry. I woke up that morning and realised how I felt about you and...and it was huge. My head was all over the place and then my mother rang. She'd seen something in the paper that suggested we were a couple. That photo of us all in the park.'

Grace nodded. 'Helena showed it to me. She said that there'd been a reporter in the department pretending to be a patient. That you'd told her we were just colleagues. Friends. That it would never be anything more than that.'

She looked away from Charles. A long, pristine stretch of the wide pathway lay ahead of them, the string of lamps shining to illuminate the bare, snow-laden branches of the huge, old trees guarding this passage. The snow was still falling but it was gentle now. Slow enough to be seen as separate stars beneath the glow of the lamps.

'I'd thought I would be able to find you as soon as I got to work. That I could warn you of the media interest. I thought...that I was protecting you from having your privacy invaded by putting them off the scent. And...and it didn't seem that long. It was only a day...'

Grace squeezed her eyes shut. 'It felt like a month…'

'I'm sorry…'

The silence continued on and then she heard Charles take a deep breath.

'I can't believe I made the same mistake. For the same reasons.'

'It's who you are, Charles.' Grace opened her eyes but she didn't turn to meet his gaze. 'You're always going to try and protect your family above everything else.'

She was looking at the fountain they were approaching. She'd seen it in the daytime—an angel with one hand held out over a pond. The angel looked weighed down now, her wings encrusted with a thick layer of snow.

Their carriage driver was doing a slow circuit around the fountain. Grace felt Charles shift slightly and looked up to see him staring at the angel.

'She's the Angel of the Waters, did you know that?'

'No.'

'The statue was commissioned to commemorate the first fresh water system for New York. It came after a cholera outbreak. She's blessing the water, to give it healing powers.'

He turned to meet her gaze directly and

there was something very serious in his own. A plea, almost.

For healing?

'I do understand,' Grace said softly. 'And I don't blame you for ignoring me that first time. But it hurt, you know? I really didn't think you would do it again…'

'I didn't realise I was. I went into the pattern that I'd learned back then, to focus on protecting the people that mattered. My mother was upset. It was Thanksgiving and the family was gathering. The worst thing that could happen was to have everything out there and being raked up all over again.'

Grace was silent. Confused. He had gone to goodness only knew how much trouble to create this dream sleigh ride for her and he'd kissed her as if she was the only person who mattered. And yet he had made that same mistake. Maybe it hadn't seemed like very much time to him but it had felt like an eternity to her.

'What I said to that reporter was intended to protect you, Grace, as much as to try and keep the spotlight off my family. I had the feeling that you never talk about what you've been through. That maybe I was the only person who knew your story. I didn't want someone digging through your past and making something private public. You'd told me that that was the worst thing you could imagine happening. Especially something that was perhaps private between just *us*—that made it even more important to protect.'

He sighed as the carriage turned away from the fountain and continued its journey.

'I needed to talk to you somewhere private and it just wasn't happening. I couldn't get near you at work. There was the family Thanksgiving dinner and I was running late. I knocked on your door but you weren't home.'

'I was Skyping my dad. I couldn't answer the door.' And she could have made it easier for him, couldn't she? If she'd only had a little more confidence. She could have texted him again. Or made an effort to find him at work instead of waiting for him to come and find her.

He hadn't been put off by her scarred body. He'd been trying to protect her from others finding out about it. It made it a secret. One that didn't matter but was just between them. A private bond.

'I know that you don't actually need my protection,' Charles said slowly. 'That you're strong enough to survive anything on your own, but there's a part of me that would like you to need it, I guess. Because I want to be able to give it to you.'

They were passing the carousel now, the brightly coloured horses rising and falling under bright lights. There were children riding the horses and they could hear shrieks of glee.

'The boys are missing you,' Charles added quietly. 'They were drawing pictures for you this morning and I said that you'd love them and probably put them in a frame and Max said...he asked if you'd come back then.'

'Oh...' Grace had a huge lump in her throat.

'We need you, Grace. The boys need you. *I* need you.'

He took his hands from beneath the warmth of the blankets to cradle her face between them.

'I love you, Grace Forbes. I think I always have...

The lump was painful to swallow. It was too hard to find more than a single word.

'Same...'

'You were right in what you said—I will always protect my family above everything else. But you're part of my family now. The part we need the most.'

They didn't notice they had left the carousel

behind them as they sank into another slow, heartbreakingly tender kiss.

When Grace opened her eyes again, she found they were going past the Wollman skating rink. Dozens of people were on the ice, with the lights of the Manhattan skyline a dramatic backdrop.

'I thought I had to ignore how I felt in order to protect the people around me,' Charles told her. 'But now I know how wrong I was.'

He kissed her again.

'I want everybody to know how much I love you. And I'm going to protect that love before everything else because that's what's going to keep us all safe. You. Me. The boys...' He caught Grace's hand in his own and brought it up to his lips. 'I can't go down on one knee, and I don't have a ring because I'd want you to choose what's perfect just for you, but... will you let me love you and protect you for the rest of our lives—even if you don't need it and even if I don't get it quite right sometimes? Will you...will you marry me, Grace?

'Yes...' The word came out in no more than a whisper but it felt like the loudest thing Grace had ever said in her life.

This sleigh ride might have been a dream come true but it was nothing more than a stage set for her *real* dream. One that she'd thought she'd lost for ever. To love and be loved in equal measure.

To have her own family…

She had to blink back the sudden tears that filled her eyes. Had to clear away the lump in her throat so that she could be sure that Charles could hear her.

'Yes,' she said firmly, a huge smile starting to spread over her face. 'Yes and yes and *yes*…'

EPILOGUE

IT WAS A twenty-minute walk from the apartment block to the Rockefeller Center but the two small boys weren't complaining about the distance. It was too exciting to be walking through the park in the dark of the evening and besides, if they weren't having a turn riding on Daddy's shoulders, they got to hold hands with Grace.

'Look, Daddy...look, Gace...' It was Max's turn to be carried high on his father's shoulders. 'What are they doing?'

'Ice skating,' Charles told him. 'Would you like to try it one day soon?'

'Is Gace coming, too?'

'Yes.' Grace grinned up at the little boy, her heart swelling with love. One day maybe he would call her 'Mummy' but it really didn't matter.

'Of course she is,' Charles said. 'Remember

what we talked about? Grace and I are going to be married. Very soon. Before Christmas, even. We're a family now.'

'And Gace is going to be our *mummy*,' Cameron shouted.

Max bounced on Charles's shoulders as a signal to be put down. 'I want to hold my mummy's hand,' he said.

'She's *my* mummy, too.' Cameron glared at his brother.

'Hey…I've got two hands. One each.' Grace caught Charles's gaze over the heads of the boys and the look in his eyes melted her heart.

Mummy.

It *did* matter.

Not the name. The feeling. Feeling like the bond between all of them was unbreakable.

Family.

A branch of the Davenport family of New York—something which she still hadn't got used to—but their own unique unit within that dynasty.

Charles had shown her the Davenport ring last week, after that magical sleigh ride in the park.

'I've told Zac it's waiting for him, if he ever gets round to needing it. It belongs to the past and, even before you agreed to marry me, I knew it wouldn't suit you.'

'Because it's so flashy?'

'Because it represents everything that is window dressing in life, not the really important stuff.'

'Like love?'

'Like love. Like what's beneath any kind of window dressing.'

He'd touched her body then. A gentle reminder that what her clothes covered was real. Not something to be ashamed of but a symbol of struggle and triumph. Something to be proud of.

So she had chosen a ring that could have also made its way through struggle and triumph already. An antique ring with a simple, small diamond.

'We're almost there, guys.' Charles was leading them through the increasingly dense crowds on the Manhattan streets. 'Let's find somewhere we'll be able to see.'

Grace could hear the music now. And smell hotdogs and popcorn from street stalls. People around them were wearing Santa hats with flashing stars and reindeer antlers that made her remember the horse that had pulled her sleigh so recently on the night that had changed her life for ever.

They couldn't get very close to the Rockefeller Center in midtown Manhattan but it didn't matter because the huge tree towered above the crowds and the live music was loud enough to be heard for miles. Charles lifted Cameron to his shoulders and Grace picked up Max to rest him on her hip. He wrapped his arms around her neck and planted a kiss on her cheek.

'I love you, Mummy.'

'I love you, too, Max,' she whispered back.

A new performance was starting. If it wasn't Mariah Carey singing, it was someone who sounded exactly like her. And it was *her* song: 'All I Want for Christmas Is You'.

Grace leaned back against the man standing protectively so close behind her. She turned her head and smiled up at him.

'That's so true,' she told him. 'It's now officially my favourite Christmas song, ever.'

'Mine, too.'

When the song finished, the countdown started and when the countdown finished, the magnificent tree with its gorgeous crystal star on the top blazed into life.

The Christmas season had officially begun.

And Grace had all she had ever wanted. All she would ever want.

The tender kiss that Charles bent to place on her lips right then made it clear that they both did.

* * * * *